CW00921707

Letters from Klara

AND OTHER STORIES

Sort Of
BOOKS
www.sortof.co.uk

Letters from Klara

AND OTHER STORIES

Tove Jansson

Translated from the Swedish by

Thomas Teal

Letters from Klara (*Brev från Klara*) by Tove Jansson
This English translation first published in 2017 by

Sort Of Books
PO Box 18678, London NW3 2FL
www.sortof.co.uk

Distributed in all territories excluding the United States and Canada by

Profile Books
3 Holford Yard, Bevin Way
London WC1X 9HD

First published as *Brev från Klara* by Schildts Förlags Ab, Finland)
© Tove Jansson 1991
English translation © Thomas Teal and Sort Of Books 2017
All rights reserved

Typeset in Goudy and Gill Sans to a design by Henry Iles.
Printed in Italy by Legoprint.

 FILI   Sort of Books gratefully acknowledges the financial
assistance of FILI – Finnish Literature Exchange

144pp.
A catalogue record for this book is available from the British
Library

ISBN 978-1908745613
e-ISBN 978-1908745620

Tove Jansson's artwork for the original Swedish publication of
Brev från Klara (*Letters from Klara*), Schildts/Bonniers, 1991.

Contents

Letters from Klara

Dear Matilda,

You're hurt that I forgot your ancient birthday. You're being unreasonable. I know you've always expected me to make a special fuss, simply because I'm three years younger. But it's time you realized that the passage of years *per se* is no feather in anyone's cap.

You ask for Divine Guidance, excellent. But before it's granted, it might be a good idea to discuss certain bad habits, which, by the way, I am no stranger to myself.

Matilda, my dear, it's important to remember not to grumble if you can possibly help it. It gives those around you an immediate advantage. I know that you enjoy amazingly good health – thank your lucky stars – but you have a singular capacity to give people a bad conscience by whining, and they pay you back by becoming jovial and treating you as if you no longer mattered. I've seen it. Whatever you want or don't want, couldn't you just shout it out? Shake them up with some strong words, ruffle their feathers or, best of all, scare them a little? I know you can do it. You never knuckled under in the old days. Far from it.

And that stuff about not being able to sleep at night. Maybe because we take catnaps eight times a day? Yes, I know. Memory works backwards at night, gnawing its way through every little thing and every last tiny detail in reverse order – the times we lost our nerve, made the wrong choice, said something tactless or insensitive, were criminally unobservant – and all the social disasters, the *faux pas*, the irreparably idiotic remarks that everyone else has long since forgotten! It's so unfair to be blessed with a crystal-clear memory this late in the day! And backwards!

Dear Matilda, write and tell me what you think about these delicate matters. I promise I'll try not to be a know-all. Now don't deny it, I know that's what you think, you've said so. But I really would like to hear what you do when, for instance, you can't remember how many times you've told someone the same thing. Do you start with, "Well, as I've said before ..." or, "As I may already have mentioned ..." or what? Do you have any other suggestions? Do you just keep quiet?

And do you allow a conversation to pass right over your head? Do you try to come up with a sensible comment and realize they've changed the subject? Do you save face by insisting that they're just talking stuff and nonsense? And are we genuinely interested in what they're saying? Or curious? Please tell me that we are!

If you write to me, don't use your antediluvian fountain pen; it makes your handwriting impossible to read and moreover it's hopelessly old-fashioned. Make them get you a felt pen, medium point 0.5 mm. They have them everywhere.

Yours,
Klara

PS I read somewhere that anything written with a felt pen becomes illegible after about forty years. How about that? Lovely, don't you think? Or are you contemplating writing a memoir – you know, "not to be read for fifty years"? (Hope you think that's funny.)

♦♦♦

Dear Ewald,

Such a pleasant surprise to get your letter! Whatever gave you the idea?

Yes of course we should get together. As you say, it's been so long. It must be nearly sixty years.

Thank you for all the kind things you wrote – maybe a bit too kind, dear friend. Don't tell me you've grown sentimental?

Yes, I think growing roses is an excellent idea! Every Saturday morning on the radio they have what I'm told is a very practical programme about gardening, repeated on Sunday. You should listen to it.

Call whenever it's convenient, and remember it can take me a while to get to the phone. Don't forget to say whether you're still a vegetarian as I'm planning to make us quite a special dinner.

Yes of course you must bring your photo album. I'm hoping we can get through the inevitable "Remember whens" without too much trouble and then just talk about whatever occurs to us.

Warm regards
Klara

♦♦♦

Hi Steffe!

Thank you for the bark boat, it's very handsome, and I was so happy to get it. I tried it out in the bathtub and it balanced perfectly.

Don't worry about that bad grade. Tell your papa and mama that sometimes it's much more important to be able to work with your hands and make something beautiful.

I'm sorry about your cat. But if a cat gets to be seven-teen years old, she's probably pretty tired and doesn't feel well. Your epitaph isn't bad, but you need to take a bit more care with the rhythm. I'll explain better when I see you.

Your godmother,
Klara

♦♦♦

Dear Mr Öhlander,

According to your letter of 27 August, you suppose me to be in wrongful possession of a picture you painted in your youth, which you now seem to require as quickly as possible for inclusion in a retrospective exhibition of your work.

I have no recollection of "wheedling" the canvas from your niece's son in the course of a visit to his flat. What seems more likely is that he quite spontaneously pressed me to take it with me as I left.

I have now made a close study of the signatures on the art works in my home and have managed with difficulty to identify one that might possibly be yours. The painting seems to depict something halfway between an interior and a landscape, with leanings towards the semi-abstract.

The dimensions, which you didn't mention, are the classic French, 50 cm x 61 cm.

I will send you your picture at once and hope that in future it will enjoy a permanent place in your collection.

Klara Nygård

Dear Niklas,

You've only just come back from your "undisclosed destination" (which I strongly suspect was Mallorca). Be that as it may, I've been thinking about making another small alteration to my will. Don't groan. I know that deep down you're rather amused by all this toing and froing.

So, in short, I'm considering giving an annuity to the Retirement Home whose services I will eventually require. But please note, they get it only as long as I'm alive. I'm talking here about bank and bond interest and whatever else I can live without – which you know better than I. They can use the money any way they like.

The idea – as I'm sure you understand, cunning as you are – is that, with this income in mind, the Home will try to keep me alive as long as possible. I will be their mascot and will be allowed certain obvious liberties. Whatever is left when I die will be distributed exactly as specified earlier.

I will only add that I am at the moment in excellent health and hope you are the same.

Klara

♦♦♦

My dear Cecilia,

How nice of you to send my old letters, a dreadfully big box. Did you at least get help carrying it to the post office? I'm quite touched that you saved them (and even numbered the letters), but my dear, the thought of reading through them all! You know what I mean? The stamps were cut off for some child's collection I suppose. If you have other correspondence from the turn of the century, remember to save the whole envelope – much more desirable to philatelists. And remember to take extra care with blocks of four.

I assume you're getting rid of stuff, a perfectly natural and commendable activity. I've been doing it myself and have gradually learned a thing or two. One of them is that the little treasures you try to give young people just make them uncomfortable – more and more polite and more and more uncomfortable. Have you noticed that?

You know what? There's now a flea market on Sandvik Square every Sat and Sun. What do you think of that? People can wander around and find stuff for themselves and no one has to feel ill at ease or grateful. Brilliant idea.

You write that you've grown melancholy, but Cecilia, that's just part of getting old, it's nothing to worry about. I read somewhere that it's a physiological phenomenon, doesn't that sound comforting? Okay, you get sad, so you just sit down and tell yourself, aha, this doesn't count, it's not my fault, it just happens. See what I mean?

What else do I have to tell you? Oh yes, I have freed myself from my houseplants and I'm trying to learn some French. You know, I've always admired the way you speak it so perfectly. How do you put it, that elegant thing at the end of a letter – Chère madame, I enclose you, no, myself, in your – oh, you know how it goes.

I'm only a beginner.

Chère petite madame, I do miss you sometimes ...

Your Klara

♦♦♦

Dear Sven Roger,

I noted with gratitude that the tile stove is working again. If those bureaucrats come back and insist that it's illegal, I intend to consult my solicitor. As we all know, that stove is Historic.

When you come back from your holiday you will find that Mrs Fagerholm one flight up has cleaned out her attic storage space – long overdue – but she placed her unspeakable possessions right in front of my locker, so I quite naturally moved everything out into the corridor.

I remember you said once that you'd like to have some houseplants for your summer cottage, so I have set out my collection in a row beside the bins. Take whatever you like and throw the rest in with the rubbish. In the meantime, I'll continue to water them every evening just to be on the safe side. As an explanation of my apparently heartless behaviour, I'd just like to say that these houseplants have weighed on my conscience for years. I always seem to water them too much or too little, and I never know which.

By the way, I think we can wait to wash the windows. At the moment, they're covered with what looks like a light mist. It has a lovely effect, which we shouldn't disturb.

With friendly summer greetings,
K. Nygård

PS Don't say anything to old lady Fagerholm. I really enjoyed throwing out all her old junk.

♦♦♦

Camilla Alleén
"Just Between Us Women"

Dear Miss Alleén,

Thank you for your kind letter. But I'm afraid that I find myself unable to take part in your survey of, as you put it, the problems and pleasures of old age.

Of course I could always write that old age is difficult
yet quite interesting. But why dwell on the obvious
drawbacks? And the interesting part seems to me a very
private matter, unsuited to generalization.

My dear Miss Alleén, I'm afraid that you will not get
particularly honest answers to your questionnaire.

Yours sincerely
Klara Nygård

Robert

AT THE ART ACADEMY, we had a classmate named Robert. Robert was tall and thin and held his large head a little to one side, as if weary or lost in thought. He was very quiet and, as far as I could tell, had no friends in our class.

Robert painted very slowly. He almost never finished his canvases. Instead, he'd cover them with white and start over – and then do the same thing again.

But once in a while he'd sign one. When Robert signed a painting, we were all very aware of it. We didn't look his way, but we knew what he was doing. He signed his name with the same meticulous attention to detail, mixing the colours for the letters again and again and wiping them away. His picture was not to be sullied by anything that was not an organic part of the work, of its perfection. When Robert had finally managed to achieve the effect he wanted, we could all start working again. At that time, we did not sign our paintings.

One day I got a letter from Robert. He'd left it on my easel. It was very formal.

You are a happy person, with a happiness that seems lighthearted. As far as I can see you prefer to like people because it's easier than disliking them. I have observed you. You soar above things rather than climb over them or tunnel through – or wait.

I wish you no ill, on the contrary. Please believe in my sincerity. But I must inform you that for a variety of reasons, which are entirely private, I feel compelled to end our acquaintance.

With greatest respect,
Robert

♦♦♦

I didn't understand. The letter made me uneasy. I wasn't worried for him, no, I was more hurt than concerned. Had I ever even spoken to him? Scarcely.

Then one day as we were all crossing the courtyard to our art history lecture, he caught up to me and said, "Did you understand?" And I said, "Maybe not completely ..." I was embarrassed. Robert walked on past me across the courtyard.

What was I supposed to say? If he had tried to explain, if he'd even wanted ... I mean, that's no way to behave! But I suppose I could have asked him.

It came out gradually that Robert had written to everyone in our painting class and that every letter concluded with a very polite severance of relations. We didn't show the letters to each other, and we didn't discuss it. Maybe we thought it was a little odd to renounce something that hadn't actually existed, but we didn't say so. Everything went on as before, exactly as before.

Then came the time when we began to sign our canvases. And very soon after that came the war.

♦♦♦

One day years later, after the war, I happened to run into a classmate from art school, and we went to a café. After chatting for a while I found myself asking about Robert. "Do you know where he is these days?"

"No one knows. He got lost during the war. Walked over the border."

"What do you mean?"

"It was so like him," he went on. "You know, he just went the wrong way. It was that in-between time when nothing was happening. We just waited, whittled stuff out of wood, or whatever it was we did to kill time. Robert was filling a sketch pad, walking around in the woods and coming back to the canteen with his sketches. I think he was headed for the canteen that day too – they set a pretty good table. But he went the wrong way. He had no sense of direction."

I've thought about Robert a great deal, perhaps most of all about his farewell letter. I think I understand, now, that those letters were written from a deep need, and that they left behind an enormous sense of relief and liberation. Did he write the same kind of letter to other

people, outside of school? Did he write to his parents?
Yes, definitely to his parents.

Imagine having the nerve to push everyone away –
whether they're unreachable or you've allowed them to
come too close: "... for a variety of reasons, which are
entirely private, I feel compelled ..."

But of course you just can't.

In August

ONE EVENING IN AUGUST, Aunt Ada and Aunt Ina sat on the enclosed veranda of their villa, catching their breath. The last of their relatives had driven away and now the only sound was the wind in their garden. It was a very warm evening, but they couldn't open the windows. The moths would fly at the lamp, and killing them as they lay there beside it, trembling wings above a great hairy body, was nasty.

"Did it go well?" Ina asked. "There were too many of them. And why did they bring the younger children? I mean, it was a *memorial* service. We forgot the salad."

Ada didn't answer, and her sister went on. "Why do *we* have to do it every year, right on the anniversary of her death? Let them do it, it's easier in town. What was it that went wrong?"

"Nothing," Ada said. "Nothing at all except that you made them all uncomfortable. You talked too much about Mama. Why do you try to give them a bad conscience? Let them forget. She was terribly old, and she went quickly."

A moth had managed to get in and burn its wings on the lamp.

"Let me," said Ada quickly, and she crushed the insect with a coffee cup.

"Blow out the lamp!" Ina said.

When it was dark on the veranda, the garden came closer, silhouettes of trees moving in the night breeze.

"But I don't want them to forget," Ina said. "Why should I be the only one who remembers!"

"How do you know what they remember?" Ada said. "Anyway, they mostly saw her on the weekends. That business with the bathroom ceiling upsets them."

"And it serves them right, Ada, it serves them right! There she was, all by herself ..."

"Yes, yes, I know. Wilful, independent, and, as usual, secretive. She didn't trust anyone but herself, so she climbed up on a *stepladder* to paint the bathroom ceiling and fell off and broke her neck. She was over eighty. A good exit. And now you give me a sermon about how we should have done God knows what to give her another ten years! Ina, you know yourself that deep down she was very, well ... very ..."

"Not at all," Ina said. "Not a bit of it!" She jumped up and started pacing up and down the veranda. "She wasn't a tyrant!"

"But I never said she was."

"But that's what you meant!"

"Sit down," Ada said. "Sit down for God's sake and cool off. I know what it is you can't ever manage to say, so let's get it out in the open for once. Remember what

it was like? 'What's she doing now? What's she up to?
Why is she so quiet? Doesn't she feel well? Or did I hurt
her feelings? What is it I said or didn't say or didn't do?'
Neither one of us has forgotten the way it was. But what
difference does that make now?

"You're so hard," Ina said. "Mama was wonderful."

"Sit down."

"Ada, you remember I got a toothache when it
happened, and the doctor said it was only because I was
clenching my teeth all the time."

"I know. You told me. Sit down. I don't have the
strength to deal with you any more – and neither do you.
Now don't start crying. I'll go get some candles."

Ada came back with two lit candles and put them on
the table. She said, very pleasantly, "Ina, could anyone
have died more conveniently, and without its being a
single person's fault? She had fun. Do you understand
that? Fun! And she never had to get seriously old. She
was into a new age of rebellion, and what could we have
done about that?"

Now Ina was crying.

"Yes, yes, there, there," her sister said. "What is it you
want? Maybe you want to believe that you should have
painted that ceiling. It's still stained and half finished
and I'll bet you close your eyes when you go to brush
your teeth. Do you think you're *required* to have a bad
conscience? Are you even entitled to one?"

"Now who's preaching sermons?" Ina said. "And you
always know better than everyone else, just like Mama!
Can't I even grieve in peace?"

"Fine. Go right ahead. Be my guest. Here's a handkerchief. Ina. Think about it. It's so simple. Mama always wanted to do things herself, and she always got in ahead of everybody and didn't trust anyone else. That's the truth."

"Of course she trusted people," Ina said.

"How do you mean?"

"She trusted us to leave her in peace."

"That's good," Ada said. "Excellent. And we did leave her in peace. That's the best thing you've said for a very long time."

"You really mean it?"

"Yes, I mean it. Dear Ina, don't you think we could go to bed now?"

"You go on. I'm going to stay up for a bit."

"And you'll make sure to blow out all the candles?"

"Funny," Ina said. "Now where have I heard that before? Yes. I'll blow them out when I blow them out."

That night an odd thing happened in the elderly sisters' villa. One of them had climbed up on a stepladder to paint the bathroom ceiling, fallen off and broken her arm and two ribs. Two candles were still burning on the bathroom shelf. But the most remarkable part was that the poor woman was in such a good mood after the accident, absolutely elated. It must have been shock.

The Lily Pond

THEY HAD RENTED THE SUMMER HOUSE primarily because it stood beside a lily pond and they'd been told that their vacation would come just when the water lilies bloomed. Moreover, there was a small sauna they could use if they bought their own firewood. There were spruce trees on three sides of the house, making a dark green wall that shut out the world. It was hard to believe that a road with a bus passed just a stone's throw from the place. It would be their first summer together.

Kati had never met Bertil's mother, she had just seen pictures of her and admired her aristocratic profile and white hair. He assured her that Mama had no objection to their living together. "Kitten," he said, "she's very modern, I might almost say young at heart! You'll see!"

One week before they were to leave, Bertil's mother felt a little faint, as she put it, and wandered around her apartment not knowing what she was looking for. When he wanted to help, she just sat down, looked at him, smiled and said, "Oh, Little Squirrel, don't bother … Mama Squirrel is feeling a little faint. It will pass."

Bertil grew more and more concerned. Days passed and she didn't get better, quite the reverse. Finally, he had to discuss the situation with Kati. Kati questioned him matter-of-factly. Could his mother get along by herself for three weeks? No. Could she manage with home-care help? No …

"Kati, my little Kitten," Bertil burst out, "this isn't easy for me!"

"No, of course it isn't. This hasn't been easy for Tomcat."

"And why does it have to happen right now, all of a sudden?" he went on. "She doesn't stub out her cigarettes properly, they lie around everywhere, still smouldering. She can't remember whether she's taken her medicine several times a day or not at all!"

"And what would happen", Kati asked, "if she took her pills several times or skipped them completely?"

When Bertil didn't answer, she said, "Tomcat, have her come with us. It's high time I met your mother anyway."

And he said, "I love you, thank you, thank you, Kitten!"

Bertil and his mother climbed off the bus at the crossroads and took the short path through the woods. Kati had dinner ready. Bertil had brought wine and a bouquet of flowers for each of the ladies. He was in high spirits and told stories all through dinner. When it was quiet, his mother turned to him and said, "But my Little Squirrel hasn't put out the ashtray!" And he replied in the same caressing voice, "But Mama Squirrel smokes far too much ..." He lit her cigarette and she gave his hand a playful little smack and said, "Now, now, let's not exaggerate ..." Kati put out an ashtray, cleared the table, and served the coffee.

Day after day, these tiny rituals continued, a kind of teasing that Bertil and his mama had been rehearsing for so long that they played their parts without being aware of what they were doing. They had rituals that consisted of intimations, unfinished remarks that alluded to their long life together and entwined them in an inaccessible cocoon of memories, sometimes only a couple of words, a little laugh, a sigh, a touch of the hand.

"Kati," said Bertil, "do you think Mama is enjoying herself?"

"I certainly think so," Kati said. "But where did you get that squirrel business?"

"I could do the dishes," Bertil said. "There must be more to do with three instead of two."

"Not at all," she said. "Provided you two just stay outdoors as much as possible. Now that the weather is so nice."

Bertil had bought some garden furniture in bright, shiny colours and a garden umbrella. He'd set it all up on the lawn sloping down to the lily pond.

"Why don't they ever bloom, those lilies?" Mama wondered, and Kati replied that they would bloom very soon, any day now.

"It's important to me that they bloom," Mama said. "Ask Bertil to come here."

And Kati saw through the window how they sat whispering – definitely whispering – under the umbrella.

The beautiful weather continued.

"Little Squirrel," Mama said, "why is she so quiet?"

"Is she? Kati? Well, maybe so ..." And Bertil straightened the umbrella and went to the shed to attend to something or other that needed his attention.

It was the start of their second week when a squirrel hopped out of the woods, ran aimlessly back and forth, then sat down a short way from Mama's chair and stared at her very attentively, or so it appeared.

"It looked at me! For a long time!" she told them. "As if it wanted something from me ... We have to feed it."

Bertil moved the squirrel's food dish closer and closer to Mama's chair, and as she sat waiting under the umbrella the cheeky, curious little animal grew more and more important to her. Finally, it came all the way up to her and ate from her hand. Bertil sat in the chair across from her, and he didn't always know if she was talking to the squirrel or to him. It became a little family joke between them.

She said, "And when will those water lilies bloom so it isn't all so black? Mama Squirrel doesn't like it black ..." She looked at Bertil and smiled mournfully.

"I know," he said. "But we can't ... It takes a long ..."

They fell silent, and the sunset made its customary way toward the spruce woods opposite, down a bright orange path across the pond.

One morning the squirrel vanished. It didn't come to its feeding place all day. Mama waited and waited, but it didn't appear and she was gripped by a depression that only Bertil could understand. He came in and said, "Kati, we have to find that squirrel for her. She had to take her medicine twice already this morning. I can't calm her down! You know, that squirrel *means* something!"

"I've noticed. Kati said. "Don't let it upset you. Old people get ideas." She turned to the stove and added, "Maybe the crows got it."

Bertil went into the woods and searched for the squirrel. He called and clucked and came back and said, "I guess it's moved away somewhere." What else could he say?

"But it *meant* something!" Mama cried. "It frightens me so!"

That made him tired, and he said, "You're being unreasonable! It has nothing to do with you. There are thousands of stupid squirrels all over the place and the only thing it means is thousands of stupid squirrels!"

Mama cried a little, very quietly, and he tried to comfort her and said he was sorry. They made up just before dinner.

That night when Bertil took Kati in his arms and whispered, "My little Kitten …" she pulled away and said, "Stop calling me that. It's childish."

The next morning, the water lilies had blossomed all across the pond. Bertil moved Mama's garden chair down closer to the water.

"Beautiful, isn't it?" Kati said, and went to get the cigarettes, matches and an ashtray.

"Let me," Bertil said, and he lit Mama's cigarette and adjusted the umbrella so the sun wouldn't shine in her eyes.

"Thank you," she said. "My Little Squirrel. You'll always take care of me, won't you?"

"Always," he said. "Always ..." And he went to the shed to attend to something or other that needed his attention.

"Dear Kati," said Mama, "I think I'd like to cool my legs. Could you help me down to the water?" When they reached the water's edge, she said, "Now you mustn't watch. I don't want anyone to see my old legs except Bertil."

Kati turned away and waited. It promised to be a very hot day. Mama took off her shoes and stockings, stuck her legs into the black water, found no bottom and groped her way a little further out, screamed, and fell flat, headlong. Kati got her ashore, quite a heavy woman, black with mud, but she hadn't swallowed very much water.

Bertil came running, threw himself down beside Mama and shouted, over and over, "Kati, what have you done?! What did you do to Mama?!"

And just then, almost like in a short story, the squirrel jumped out on the grass as if nothing whatever had happened.

After a while, Kati went to fire up the sauna. It was the only thing she could think of to do.

For the moment.

The Train Trip

BOB WAS IN THE CLASS AHEAD OF ANTON. Actually, his name wasn't Bob at all but something quite different, but for those who admired him he was Bob, short and forceful, like the crack of a bat or a punch on the arm. And he had that enviable nonchalance, that self-evident right to cordially despise the whole world. Bob did not use his position to beat up his classmates; he just shrugged his shoulders and smiled absently. His way of reducing them to absolute nothingness was perfection.

Anton in the next class down had only one wish – that Bob would notice his existence. It was a wild wish – let him see me, just look straight at me and say, "Hi, Anton." He must come to see that I have a name and that I love him.

This was when Anton began writing his book about Bob. Maybe not a book, exactly, just stories where he rescued his friend. Every evening he wrote another, volume after volume. Bob was no longer Bob but X, and he himself was Z as in Zorro. There were an infinite number of ways to rescue X from horrific situations. It was really easy – although deadly dangerous. And afterwards, he went his way with a serene smile, always the same, and X looked after him, confused, in grateful admiration. After that, it was easy to sleep.

Anton came to a story he'd been saving for a long time – their exhausted trek though the desert. Their water is all gone. A sandstorm is coming. They try to take cover under a ragged tarpaulin that gets ripped to shreds, they cling tightly to each other in order to breathe …

It's a long story. They stumble onwards, the sun hotter than ever. X can't go any further, he collapses, Z shields his friend's face with the last bits of the tarpaulin and then goes on, searching, searching desperately for water in this burning hell of sand … And, remarkably, he finds a tiny pool of water at the bottom of a deep crevice, and with infinite patience he scoops the precious drops into his canteen. He stumbles back and says, "Drink, I beg you. It's for you. You must survive."

Bob drinks. Slowly the colour in his face returns. Anton puts the compass down beside him on the sand and walks off across the sand dunes, away.

When Anton has gone this far, something unexpected happens. Bob comes striding after him, extends the canteen and says, "You have saved my life. There is a little water left. I beg you, drink it. Share it with me just as we will share our life together."

Once that story was written, it was impossible to write more. Anton tried, but he couldn't do it. No images came to him, nothing. The stories about Bob must be

destroyed. The building had no incinerator in the courtyard, and ripping them to pieces would be barbaric and,
moreover, a lot of work. Anton decided that all of it
should vanish in the sea, the same way that he hoped
his ashes would be spread some day on the bounding
main (preferably the Atlantic). He went up to the attic
for a suitcase and filled it with everything he'd written.
It was very heavy when full, so he took the bus to the
harbour. It was a Sunday, the ice had broken up and
the sun was shining. Anton walked out to the end of
the point, put some stones in the suitcase, and heaved
it into the sea as far out as he could. Then he turned at
once and walked back.

The suitcase sank down to the bottom and there, very
slowly, it began coming apart at the seams, because it
was a wartime suitcase, made of camouflaged cardboard.
Notebook after notebook, filled with writing from cover
to cover, floated out into the harbour, but a friendly
breeze carried them over to Tallinn, maybe even further.

Twenty years later, an early morning in March, Anton
took the train north. He was on his way to congratulate
the family's faithful old maidservant on her ninetieth
birthday in the village where she was born. He had
with him a beautifully decorated album of family photo-
graphs with his own verses, neatly hand-printed. Anton
worked at a firm that specialized in greeting cards – cards
for weddings, births, condolences, every kind of recurring event – plus some with small humorous verses that
offered disarming apologies for lateness, say, or some
social *faux pas*. The job amused Anton. He had put his

album into a black attaché case. He hoped to complete the presentation in time to catch the night train home.

The northbound train came in. He walked from carriage to carriage until he found a non-smoker, and there sat Bob, reading his morning paper. Bob, broader in the face, heavy under the eyes, but with the same expression of indulgent disdain. Now he lowered his paper and said, "Dr Livingstone, I presume? Have we met?"

"I was in the class below you," Anton said, putting down his case. He sat opposite Bob. It was terribly hot in the car.

"And your name is?"

"Anton."

"Yes, of course. How time flies. We don't exactly get younger, do we?" Bob said, and laughed.

His teeth are just as white. He is so tanned you might think he'd come straight from the tropics. It's the first time we've ever spoken to each other. Now he'll say, "And what are you up to these days," and Bob said those very words, and Anton answered quickly.

"I'm a writer."

"Never would have guessed. Can you make any money writing books?" Bob lit a cigarette but put it out almost immediately and said how awful it tasted the morning after.

It was really unbearably hot. Anton tried to raise the window but couldn't get it open.

"Let me," Bob said. "See? Easy peasy."

The ground was still covered with snow, but the wind had blown it from the trees.

"Look here, Alan," Bob said. "As I said, last night was kind of a late night. I think I need a little hair of the dog." He opened his black business case and took out a leather-covered flask. "From Tibet," he said. "Genuine. It was part of a deal. Bottoms up. I'll feel better in a minute."

It was quiet for a while, then Anton said, "And what about yourself?"

"Just dandy. Buying and selling. Sometimes up, sometimes down. Big deals. You know, our man in Havana, our man in Haparanda!" He laughed again, and a few moments later he said, "I'm tired."

"Why don't you sleep for a while?"

"Good idea," Bob said. "You're a nice guy. If only it wasn't for your eyes, those damned puppy-dog eyes that followed me everywhere … Scoot over." He put his feet up on the seat across from him and fell asleep at once.

The long Finnish landscape went by outside, forest on both sides, nothing but forest, further and further north, hour after hour.

Bob woke up. "You look awful," he said. "Are you feeling sick too?"

"Yes, I am," Anton said. "All these damned pine trees, on and on, all the same, all the time. It's enough to make anyone sick."

"That's good!" Bob exclaimed. "Alan, you're funny! Pine trees, pine trees, pine trees! Now let's have another snort and then go get something to eat. I could eat a horse."

He liked that. I was funny. Although actually I've always really liked pine trees …

It was fascinating to watch Bob eat, slowly and with undisguised pleasure. Just like before. Like everything he did – lying stretched out on the school playground in the spring sunshine, showering after a football game, running faster, jumping higher – he was on good terms with his body, his sleep, his food, everything …

There was a silence, and Anton asked the easiest question:

"Do you ever see any of them?"

"No, why should I? I quit in the sixth. And anyway, who cares? Why not just forget about them. You know, it's like you're some kind of old pine tree with dead branches clinging on at the bottom, you know, what's the word, obseek …"

"Obsequious?" Anton suggested.

"Right. This coffee tastes like shit. Wait a second." Bob took his flask from his pocket. "They don't even have booze on this train … And your obsequious eyes. They were on me all the time. You followed me every-where. You know what, Alan? They laughed at me. Ha ha, you've got a little admirer! God what a pain."

"Anton," said Anton. "Not Alan."

"You were like a puppy trying to ingratiate itself, begging to be beaten. Did you get a beating? No. Never from me. Attacking a little kid, skinny and weak – I don't do that."

"Be quiet for a minute," Anton burst out. "How was I supposed to know what it felt like for you? Okay, okay, of course, I was annoying, childish, comical, but what do you expect? Didn't you ever have an idol, some kind of superman, someone even stronger than you? Who did *you* worship in those days?"

"Don't make a scene," Bob said. He hadn't been listening. He sat there playing with his napkin, folding it into smaller and smaller squares, then he crumpled it up and threw it on the floor. "Funny," he said. "Somehow everything gets smaller and smaller ... Now listen to me, this is what I've been thinking. I've been thinking that if you admire somebody, you think you have the right to own them, you own the other person. Do you get what I'm saying? You use him, somehow. And he can't do anything about it. Isn't that right?"

"Yes," Anton said.

"Good. I was right. And how much fun do you think that is? It's shitty. You never feel free."

"Trying to live up to expectations!" said Anton rather sharply.

"No, no, not at all. Don't be dumb. But you're being watched, you know, all the time. I suppose no one has ever admired you, so you can't understand what it's like. Now let's have another little drink and forget the whole thing, just draw a line through it, as if nothing happened. Okay? I got this flask in Tibet. Genuine."

"No," Anton said. "You got it in a business deal. You said so. You've never been in Tibet. And you use a tanning lamp."

"Whoops," said Bob. "Someone's feelings got a little hurt." He laughed good-naturedly and raised his glass to his travelling companion. "You know what? It happens to some people all the time and others not at all. Know what I mean? What time is it? Left my watch at home. Never mind, doesn't matter."

Right now, right then, in the schoolyard I should have attacked him, blindly, fearlessly, and settled accounts with him. I really should have.

"Shall we go back?" Anton said.

"Yes, yes," Bob said, "but you know you can never really go back ... You were so little, a nothing, a little nothing. When you start out, everything is a nothing, isn't it? Unless you're nothing but eyes ..."

"Come on, let's go," Anton said.

"But I have to pay."

"It's all taken care of. Let's go."

"Fine," Bob said. "Very good. Excellent. Have I got my case?"

"No, we left it behind."

"Very careless, very, very careless ..." Bob got to his feet. The train shook and jerked. Between cars they were walking on screeching metal plates. It was a very old train. An outside door was open, slamming back and forth.

"Anton!" Bob shouted. "The door!"

Anton grabbed hold of him and they were thrown against the wall. Bob's whole body was shaking. "Hold on to me," Bob said. "Don't let go."

Outdoors, it had snowed. The spruces trees were completely white. Anton closed the door. They got back to their seats.

"I need some water," Bob said.

Anton went to the lavatory and filled the empty flask with water.

Bob fell asleep immediately and slept for several hours. He didn't wake up even when the train stopped and Anton got off with his attaché case. It was a very small station, a long way from Ida's town. The train stopped for only a minute or two, then whistled and went its way.

Anton sat down on the bench outside the station. The silence was absolute. It was warm in the sun, and nothing seemed terribly important. He would send Ida a telegram and travel on with the next train, whenever it came.

When Anton opened his case, a bunch of papers fell out in the snow – glossy brochures. The case was divided into compartments for samples, textiles, price lists, and a special section for hand-painted ties with Hawaiian scenes. He put everything back and closed the case.

Actually, and in many ways, it wasn't so different from his own.

Party Games

ONE MORNING IN JANUARY, Nora read in the paper that the Swedish Girls' Lyceum had closed, and in a moment of nostalgia she decided to organize a class reunion. It wasn't easy to find her old classmates. Most of them had married and changed their names a couple of times and a few had simply disappeared or died. But Nora kept at it, approaching the problem roughly the way she attacked one of the intricate crossword puzzles she did to amuse herself these days, and by and by she had assembled a handful of ladies who promised, reluctantly, to attend. Nora decided the reunion should take place at Eva's place. Eva thought the decision was rather hasty, but she didn't object because she remembered very well that opposition was pointless once Nora started bossing people around.

Just before they all arrived, Eva put out a tray of Bloody Marys to get the ball rolling, and she softened the lighting.

They were a small group – Nora, Pamela, Edith, Kitty, Vera and Ann-Marie – but they all arrived at once and there was great confusion in the front hall as they tried to remove their winter coats and boots and simultaneously give each other hugs, plus several of them had bouquets of flowers that had to be unwrapped. And their faces did not immediately fall into place. Nora was unaltered, having only become much larger.

"Aha," she said. "Bloody Marys. Eva Specials, very explosive!"

Everyone laughed, waiting for one of the little speeches Nora had always loved to make at class parties, but Nora merely raised her glass and looked at Eva.

"Welcome," said Eva awkwardly. "It's been a long time ..." And she thought angrily that if you're going to act superior and make decisions, then you can also help out even if it takes a little effort, and in a moment of great astonishment, Eva realized that she must have disliked Nora quite a lot.

"Such a lovely apartment," Vera said.

Ann-Marie said, "Can you give me your recipe for Bloody Marys? You use pepper, don't you?"

"Yes indeed. Tabasco and vodka and a little pepper."

Ann-Marie nodded solemnly. "Pepper," she said. "Of course."

They all fell silent ...

"Well," said Pamela, "so here we sit." She turned to Vera. "And what have you been up to lately?" she asked.

"Nothing special," Vera said, digging in her handbag.

"I've got some cigarettes here someplace," Eva said. "Do you smoke?"

"Thank you, but I never have."

"So strange, all of it," Kitty said to no one in particular. "I kept thinking that I should give it a try, but somehow it never happened ..."

They all fell silent again.

Eva dived in. "Do you remember ..." she began. "Do you remember that time, we were in the eighth form, I think ..." And so they saved the day by fleeing into their inevitable schoolgirl memories and talked excitedly and called each other Ami and Stride and Squeaky. They experienced a kind of liberating rejuvenation, a recovery of girlishness. They ate and drank and got used to each other's new faces. Nora sat in a rocking chair and kept it slowly rocking. She had really grown extremely large. She looked at the others and said very little.

Suddenly Kitty said, "You know what? We all gave each other silly nicknames, but Nora was always just Nora, the queen. Why was that? And what shall we do now? Nora, you need to organize this party. I just know you can. How about we take turns telling about ourselves – whether or not we're married, have jobs – you know, very briefly, and then we'll know all about each other."

"But Kitty!" Vera burst out. "You're not angry, are you?"

"Not at all, I just know how it'll be. Someone's won the lottery and someone else's had an operation or taken a charter flight to Madeira, and then we'll talk about nothing but lotteries and surgeries and trips abroad and nothing else for hours."

Pamela said, "So now we're not allowed to talk about all that? Why are you being like this?"

"How about some coffee?" Eva said, and Vera cried, "But how about a game? A party game. Nora?"

Nora got up from her rocking chair and clapped her hands. "Girls, girls," she said, "I've got an idea."

"Quiet down, class!" Kitty shouted. "Nora has an idea! Ta-dah!"

Eva laid a cautionary hand on Kitty's arm, and Nora went on.

"Do you all remember the one about the burning house and who should I rescue first?"

"Oh, I don't think so," Edith said. "Whoever you rescued it was somehow wrong."

Kitty put up her hand and said in a baby voice, "Teacher, teacher! Can't we play that fun game where someone goes out of the room and the others say what they really think?"

She's not drunk, Eva thought. She's beside herself. What should I do?

"Last class before Christmas!" Nora shouted jokingly. "You can all have fun and talk as much as you like! Here's a good game. What would you do if you knew that you had just so much longer to live?" She sat back down in the rocking chair.

"Fascinating," said Vera, cautiously.

"How much longer do we have?" Pamela wanted to know.

"Decide for yourselves," Nora said.

"A week?"

"No," Ann-Marie said, "that doesn't give you enough time to do anything."

"Six months?" Edith suggested.

Vera said, "But that's enough time to get scared."

They agreed on a month, pens and paper were passed around, and each of them was to put what she'd written on the table in front of Eva, without a name. She sat and looked at them as they wrote, so obedient and earnest, and wondered why it was that extremely reserved people revealed themselves so freely the moment they were playing a parlour game. She thought about college examinations – what do you know about … ? what can you say about … ? – and you had less than an hour to answer.

Now they came over to her, one after another, and left their folded papers on the table.

"Read," Nora said.

"*I'd clean the house.*"

"But you'd do that anyway," Ann-Marie burst out. "And for that matter, in a month it would be dirty again! Does she say anything else?"

"*And burn all the letters that could make anyone unhappy.*"

"Good!" Kitty shouted. "Teacher? Nora? You have to give her a grade. Ten!"

"Negative nine," Nora said. "Her reasoning is obvious and not original. Eva, read on."

"*I would figure out what I've always longed to do and then do it, heedlessly, thinking only of myself.*"

Edith: "But you can't change careers in one month …"

Ann-Marie: "But shouldn't she tell us what it is she longs to do?"

"She doesn't know yet," Vera said, and Nora interrupted. "We'll get into all of that later. Eva, read the next one."

"This one has a very ugly picture. And underneath it, a lot of writing that's been crossed out in black."

"It's Kitty's!" Edith shouted.

"No, it's not mine."

"Can we look at the picture?" Pamela said.

But Eva continued. *"To feel like a balloon that's lost its string. To be wide awake and see everything differently. To be unable to comprehend how others can go on without you. Isn't that good?"*

"Yes, indeed," Nora said. "But it's off the subject. She hasn't written about what she would do but about how it would feel. We have to stick to the rules."

"You and your rules," Edith said, and everyone started talking at once. Eva unfolded a piece of paper that was blank, then she stood up to go and get the coffee, nodded to Kitty and they went into the kitchen together.

"Stop crying," Eva said. "They'll go home soon and it will all be over."

Kitty sat down on the kitchen counter. "Of course it's not over," she said. "I can't get them out of my head, those awful games. "A-Tisket, A-Tasket", and nobody picked me, and everyone pointed, left out! And children are supposed to think that's fun?!"

"I remember," Eva said. "It was cruel. But it was such a long time ago."

Kitty wasn't listening. She went on. "And then those intelligence games. Nora's quizzes. Eva, forget the coffee for a second and listen to me. You weren't allowed to save yourself and quit because then you were chicken, a bad loser!"

"Yes, it was awful. Now I'm taking in the coffee. Kitty, dear, bring in the other tray, but carefully. The class gave me that decanter when I graduated, remember? It was Nora picked it out."

"I'm sure she did," Kitty said. "Do you know what my uncle said once about a really ugly glass carafe? Wait, don't go! Can you forgive me if I say something nasty to Nora? It won't ruin your party?"

"Do you have to?"

"Yes, I think I do."

"Well, then say it, for heaven's sake," Eva said and carried in the coffee. She was tired.

"No cognac for me," Pamela said. "I'll just take some liqueur."

"That's much stronger," Kitty said. "You know nothing about spirits. But just look at this splendid glass carafe! It was Nora picked it out. Who else? Forty years ago, and no one has ever had the nerve to break it. Nora! Would you like to know what my uncle said about a glass carafe? At a family gathering? He said, 'Have you ever seen a rooster pee in a glass carafe?'!"

"But good heavens," Pamela said, "what could he have meant by that?"

"Wanted to shock them," Nora explained amiably. "He probably just needed to let off steam. But dear Kitty, no one's shocked these days by childish scatological remarks. How old was he when he died, your uncle?"

"Ninety-two."

Now she's going to start crying again, Eva thought. And how am I going to get them to go home?

"Speaking of death," said Ann-Marie quickly, "have you all seen how they don't have proper crosses on the death notices in the paper any more? Some of them have birds and palm fronds and all sorts of things ..."

"They're just putting on airs," Edith said. "And what does it have to do with us?"

The wind had come up, and when the room was quiet they looked out at the storm that was throwing snow against the windowpanes. Someone said it might be hard to get a taxi, and who should it take home first, and suddenly everything was back to normal.

"We'll need two," Nora said, and Eva said that she'd planned a little hot dish before they left. Everyone got up and started searching for their purses and glasses and cigarettes. Nora raised her great weight from the rocking chair and said, "We've stayed far too long, it's really time for us to go. It's been a fine evening, Eva. Kitty, your purse is right there."

"I know perfectly well where my purse is!" Kitty said. "Don't be so bossy. Shall I tell you more about my uncle? Do you know what he said? 'Do what you like and make yourselves happy. Go to bed with your boots on and empty your chamber pots right out the window!'"

"Yes, why not," said Nora thoughtfully. She studied Kitty for a moment and went on. "Have you all said goodbye and have you got everything? Eva, can you call the taxi? Get two, and ask them to back into the entryway. The pavement is icy."

Eva stood with the receiver at her ear, waiting for taxi central to answer. It rang and rang. She reached out her hand and pulled Nora closer so they were both waiting for the connection.

"Kitty?" said Nora over her shoulder. "Just one thing. Please, would you tell me what it was you wrote on that paper? Even though it's against the rules?"

"Of course," Kitty said. "That I'd go on living my life as usual."

"Ten plus!" Nora shouted.

"Six three four," Eva repeated. "Two cars. And could you back them into the entryway?"

They said their goodbyes in the front hall, with an affection that was perfectly genuine but that committed them to nothing.

Pirate Rum

THAT SUMMER, Jonna and Mari stayed on their island into September. Every time they were ready to move back to town there was a run of hard weather and they had to unpack again, and when the weather calmed down and turned beautiful, they thought, Why not stay a little longer? And then of course some new storm blew up.

Every autumn people would worry about the elderly ladies and say this was probably the last year they'd come out.

One evening it started blowing from the east, and an east wind was always worst because the boat was too heavy to pull up on shore, so they had to anchor it out in the water with lines to hold it steady. The island was shaped like an atoll, with a lagoon in the middle, and when the seas came straight from the east, they broke over the rocky barrier in great waterfalls and roared on across the lagoon, while from the other side came waves reflected from the opposite shore, leaving the *Victoria*, held by four lines, to struggle as best she could in a little vacuum of clashing breakers. Jonna checked the lines every year and bought new shackles. If the wind rose more than normal, she added extra lines. They would stand there silently, staring at the dancing boat, then go back into the cottage.

Late that evening, something unusual happened – they had a visitor. He walked straight in without saying a word. He was very young and thin and looked angry.

"Close the door," Jonna said. "Where did you leave your boat?"

He waved his hand vaguely toward the lagoon, sat down on the floor, and put his head in his hands.

"Did you pull it up properly?"

He didn't answer. Jonna and Mari took torches and went down to look. It was a canoe, and it lay banging on the rocks. They pulled it further up.

When they got back, their guest had thrown his wet clothes on the floor and stood in front of the open stove wrapped in a blanket.

"Well," said Jonna. "A few more minutes and it would have holed its bottom. Have you no respect for your boat?"

"I'm sorry," he said. "I guess it's a little late to drop in ... Lennart Ågren. From Lovisa."

"Mari from Helsingfors," Mari said. "Didn't you listen to the weather?" She put out socks, trousers, and a sweater. "Lennart," she said, "you can change in the hall."

When she'd closed the door, Jonna told her she shouldn't start mothering him. And Mari said, "What's the matter with you? I simply don't want him getting pneumonia just as we're getting packed, that's all!"

Lennart came back in and sat down on the bed. For the first time, he studied his hosts, a long, comprehensive look. Finally he explained that they probably couldn't really understand anything as crazy as a truly desperate act, but that they really had to try.

Mari hung his wet clothes above the stove. His red shirt bore the inscription "I couldn't care less".

"Depends what you mean by desperate?" Jonna said. "What were you up to, actually, heading out into a storm in a canoe?"

Lennart answered, "I wanted to die." He stood up and started pacing furiously back and forth in the room. Then he said, "Women!"

"What did you say?" Jonna said.

"Women. What do they want, really?"

The water had started boiling and Mari poured some in his glass and told him to drink while it was still hot.

"Exactly," said Lennart. "That's what Mama always says. What is it? It smells funny."

"It's rum and water, sugar, ginger, and butter. It's called pirate rum. But don't let the butter congeal, because then it's not nice any more."

Mari put more wood in the stove and put on some potatoes.

"Food," he said. "No food for me. That's the last thing I want."

"Good," Jonna said. "We've already eaten."

"And my back hurts. Probably psychosomatic."

"Too much paddling. We brought up your paddle so it doesn't blow away. Now, please couldn't you sit down somewhere? The room seems so small with someone constantly marching back and forth."

"I'm sorry," Lennart said and sat down on the bed again. "What I said about women," he explained earnestly, "you probably don't understand what I mean. You've lived too long and too protected. It's not your fault."

"Would you like another one?" Mari asked.

"Maybe, but without the butter. What I mean is, they try to own you, organize your damned life so completely that you have no freedom at all! I realize you do your best, especially when you're old, but all the same … you can't see the big picture!"

Jonna said, "All I can see is that you went out in a canoe in a near gale. What were you thinking?"

"I wanted to die!" said Lennart angrily. "I just told you!"

"But why?" Mari said.

Jonna observed that he could just as well die tomorrow instead, since the wind just seemed to keep rising.

"You're brutal," he said.

"Really. You find a landing place. There's a light in the window, and you stumble to the house. People take care of you and they're brutal. Have I got that right?"

To their horror, Lennart started to cry, laboured, hacking sobs.

Jonna whispered to Mari, "See what you can do. I was mean."

Mari sat down beside him on the bed and waited. Finally he said, "They want to own you. Love you to death."

"Yes of course. I understand," Mari said.

"You don't understand a thing! Why can't they be nice, I mean, keep some distance, give you a chance to miss them a little, so you're happy to see them again?"

"Let's have some coffee," Jonna said.

"Shush, Jonna. We're talking. Don't fuss." Mari turned to Lennart and said, "You're right. It was your mother, wasn't it?"

He jumped to his feet and shouted, "Don't drag Mama into this!"

"No, of course not," Mari said. "Fine, fine. I think I'll go to bed now."

"Sleep," Lennart said. "Did you ever stop to think that people routinely sleep away a third of their lives? They just get into the habit of going to bed. Right? No curiosity, no imagination." He put his hand on Mari's shoulder. "Wait a bit," he said. "I want to explain something. People are like boats, we head off for a place we've been longing to visit for ages. Maybe an island. Finally we get there. And what happens? We go right past, further out. You see? We go on! Towards the unknown."

"Well," Jonna said, "it was good you didn't go on past us. You could have wound up in Estonia."

The wind had risen. Something blew down outside and clattered down the slope. Probably the paddle.

They went out and looked at the weather. The torch showed that *Victoria* was riding pretty low in the water.

"She'll make it," Jonna said.

"No," Lennart said. "That line on the east side is too taut."

"No, it's not."

"It needs another twenty centimetres at least, so the waves don't wash into the boat. Can I go do it?"

"No. You can't loosen it, and now believe me, because I know. But if you want, you can go down and check the water line. If you can't see the green, that means the accumulator is under water. Take a raincoat in the hall."

"Boy, how many times have I heard that!" Lennart burst out. "Take a raincoat, wear warm trousers, be sure you're bundled up properly and don't stay out too late!"

"Yes, my friend," Jonna said. "I had parents too."

The night had now turned coal black. They watched the torch's cone of light move down the granite slope and then stop at the water's edge.

Mari said, "What shall we do with him? What does he want?"

"He doesn't know. He's just a little despondent."

When Lennart came back, Mari had gone to bed. "I've never seen such a beautiful, gallant boat, but she's getting a beating nobody could take for very long."

"You're right," Jonna said. "But she's wood, not plastic. *Victoria* was built thirty years ago and she's as seaworthy as they come."

"Yes. That's the kind of boat I want."

"Why not? The last real boatbuilders are right in this area. I can give you an address."

"No addresses," Lennart said. "Then it's someone I have to write to."

Mari fell asleep as she half listened to them talking about boats. The conversation was very down-to-earth.

By morning, the storm had passed.

His jeans had dried. One day he'd find the boatbuilder's address in his back pocket.

About Summer

1

The sun was setting. After the storm, the water was all the way up to the boat shed. The whole meadow by the shore was flooded, and it felt funny walking across the grass with water swishing around your feet. I found an old broken barrel and rolled it down to the boat beach and turned it on end and climbed in. The grass under the water was very soft and it kept moving the whole time. I pretended I was in a submarine. The barrel had a big enough hole that I could see the sun. She was fiery and turned the walls of the barrel red. I sat there in the warm water and no one knew I was there. Nothing more happened that day.

2

I decided to make a road. If the trees were small and thin I sawed them down. The road was very twisty because it had to go around all the big trees. I worked at it every morning and it got longer and longer. I had planned to build a treehouse where the road went down to the water on the other side, high enough so they wouldn't know where I was but not so high that I couldn't look at everyone who went by down below. But it didn't turn out so good. Maybe the road was too narrow and went in a circle, because it came out almost the same place where it started. That happens. But why do people need roads anyway? I mean, we get where we're going anyway!

3

I made a secret room for myself in the attic and hammered only when I knew no one was in the house. When the room was done, I carried up the kerosene lamp from the kitchen and waited till it was dark to light it. I could see the lamp reflected in the window. They came up the attic stairs and said I couldn't do that, that I could burn the whole house down! Pretend you've got a lamp, that's what other children do when they build a house. That was too much for me. I'm not other children, I'm me, and I built a hideout. With a lamp. So I moved out.

4

For the first time I've swum in deep water and I did it by myself when no one was looking. It was four strokes, from the swimming place to the big rock. I had done enough thinking about Bottomless Depths so I just jumped in. The water was black under me, but I knew it would be. Getting across went real fast, but I started getting cold. There was a roll of birch bark on the rock and I took it back with me as proof that I'd been there. It took me six strokes on the way home. Actually, I don't think parents should let their children swim in deep water without, for example, hiding behind a rock to see they get back all right. I'm going to remember that when I have children.

5

I taught myself to row. I got up every morning before the others because I didn't want them to watch while I was learning how. You have to be very smart and stubborn. To start with, it just went around in circles. The boat is a dinghy and it's only got one thwart, which means only one board to sit on, because there wouldn't be room for any more. It is *not* made of plastic, which is very good, and it doesn't have a name. We just call it The Dinghy. When The Dinghy and I shove off from land, the sun has barely come up and it's cold. I pole my way out in the bay and start rowing. Since I'm facing the stern, not the bow, the wake is important. It's supposed to be straight, but it's not. I've noticed that I row too hard with my right oar, which is probably typical. You can pick a land-mark, which is a good thing to remember, and then keep a steady eye on your wake. We row further and further away and it gets warmer. If I keep going straight on out, we could be like a little dot that you can barely see.

They scan the horizon but decide that dot is just some eider duck and then they look in the other direction. I could teach myself to disappear. You just go on rowing, there's no end to how far you can row once you learn how. But one thing I'd like to emphasize is that when you come back, you should tie up The Dinghy properly with half hitches and take in the rowlocks. And put the oars under the thwart. You can't count on the weather. Sometime we're going to row out when it's blowing, hopefully with the wind at our backs. I know how to do it. You hold The Dinghy steady with the oars and just let it go, because the waves are coming behind you, from the stern. But that will be somewhat later.

6

On Monday, the others were in town and there was a storm that night. Hilma sleeps in the kitchen, and when she's asleep she doesn't hear a thing. I lay there under my quilt and thought about all those in peril on the sea, because that's what you're supposed to do, but in the end I only thought about me. The whole cottage was shaking. The storm surrounded the house and wanted to come in. It howled. I tried to find words for the storm. Mostly, it howls. But it can whine too, which could just be the stovepipe on the tile stove. I lifted my head so I could hear better and I came up with "shriek", the storm shrieks, that's a good word for it. It complains, that sounds right. It shouts? No, wrong. I started getting interested. I went out into the hall and opened the door just a crack but it blew wide open. Now the storm seemed far way and sounded completely different. I gave it new words: You roar. You rumble. You hiss like a cat! And sometimes you're quiet and just wait, and then you thunder! I made up my own words for the storm but now I've forgotten them. Anyway, I can make new ones next time. Because now I know how!

7

I think when I have a daughter, I'll teach her to whistle. It could be useful to whistle to each other in case we lost track of each other in the woods. If she doesn't answer, then I'll know she wants to be left alone. If she goes out in The Dinghy, I won't row after her and bring her home if it starts to blow. I won't make her pick blueberries, but she can pick mushrooms because that's fun. My daughter can wear any old trousers she wants to, and she can talk back to me, though not too much. She will look like me but prettier. Autumn is coming, so I won't write any more today.

8

I've discovered how to rhyme, it's really easy. Listen to this:

> *That old lady's such a hag*
> *She just makes me want to gag.*

I won't say who I'm thinking of.

Or how about:

> *Deep black water is a fright*
> *And it's even worse at night.*

I think that one's really good.
Or you can make it longer, for example like this:

> *I think that one day I'll declare without so much as blinking*
> *Exactly what it is I want and what it is I'm thinking.*

You just have to hum it – ta di da di da di da – and
then it comes to you. I figured that out today.

9

I've painted murals in the woodshed. It was quiet there
because they'd already chopped all the wood for winter.
The woodshed has good walls to paint on. The wood is
old and it takes red lead and net dye and tar really well.
I found brushes in the boathouse. It's very important
to put the brushes in a jar with turpentine over night.
Some people forget to do that and then they find out
what happens. I started at the top because I noticed that
when the paint runs it can make new ideas further down.
I had fun and no one came in. I painted as horrible as I
could and it turned out pretty good. As soon as you come
in you see the Loch Ness Monster rising out of the sea,
she's the biggest of them. Red paint is running out of her
mouth because she's just eaten some tourists. Above her,

near the roof, are some black fighter planes in formation, like migrating geese. It creates an Effect. In the north corner I had some ghosts, but they didn't turn out well. Maybe I'll paint over them. I put in little Monsters here and there as the paint started to dry but they're a little sketchy. This time of year the sunset comes straight in through the window and then my murals start to glow. It's kind of a shame I can't show them to anyone. But I know what would happen. Either they'd scold me or else praise me. And then it wouldn't be the same any more. Since the summer is over tomorrow, I've nailed shut the door to the woodshed. Sometimes it's good to make a decision. But I'm going to show the murals to my daughter.

The Pictures

YTTERBY LAY AT THE FAR END of the moor. The post came three times a week, and Victor's papa signed for people's registered letters, if there were any, and put everything on the veranda table where they could find their letters and newspapers whenever they came by. Otherwise, he had nothing to do with the other villagers.

The registered letter about Victor's scholarship came on a Tuesday in the first week of November.

That same evening, Papa wrote the date in his notebook, along with the following facts: "With the help of a correspondence course and thanks to the exhibition 'Young Painters' in the capital, along with an evaluation from the State Committee on Art, my son Victor has been awarded a trip abroad, including round trip fare and seven weeks' exclusive use of a private studio. Victor read the letter first and then I."

Papa put the notebook aside. A little later he took it out again and continued writing, rapidly: "My dear son, my dear distant, silent son: as you can see, I have used this notebook to make a strictly factual record of everything that has happened to you since the year after your birth, the way I suppose your mother would have done if she had not died (R.I.P.). So I have catalogued your somewhat difficult childhood (and what childhood is not difficult?), but now, because the Letter has come, I will permit myself to be a little more outspoken, in other words, to say what I mean. I love you, but I am a little tired of your remoteness and tired of the pictures that you so jealously conceal. I find the same lack of gener-osity in your silence."

Papa paused. He crossed out and started again. "I never ask and you never ask, why don't you ask, is it that too many words make you silent? In any case you could say, for example – 'Papa, your horrors don't exist, you just imagine them,' and I could defend myself and explain quite calmly and say believe me, they do exist. Have you never ever seen an apparition, the other face behind your own in the mirror, a hideous enlargement of your own conscience, no of course you haven't ... People think I'm odd, not to be taken seriously. They've never heard the footsteps that follow a person, that stop when you stop and then start again ... Are you ashamed of me? You who help them with their everyday chores, their silly henhouses ... But wait! Now everything is different, we're being set free."

Papa tore out the whole page, then shouted, "Victor! Come here! Come here, I want to talk to you."

He looked at his son, yes, they were much alike, broad

eyebrows, very light eyes, hesitant mouths. But his hair was his mother's, black.

Papa then reported, as a direct challenge, "They followed me all the way home, but I paid no attention. That annoyed them. One of them flew – very close to the ground." He observed his son intently, and he thought, Who am I bluffing, you or myself? Doesn't matter. But say something! You're getting away from here, you little bastard, but you might at least argue with me or agree that I see, that I sense these ... these companions, and without waiting for an answer, Papa continued. "I want to see your pictures. I want to look at them now, again, and take my time."

Victor said, "It's starting to get dark. You'll hardly be able to see them."

"Darkness," Papa said. "Darkness, twilight, dusk – we have more than enough of all that in this place, and that's just what I want to look at in your pictures. Whether you're painting this moor or a loaf of bread or some potatoes, they'll all be in the same damned twilight. But why do you paint such small pictures of such a large moor? And yet your moor is larger still ... Well, why don't you say something? No offence, but your bread loaves are boring. I don't know how you put life in a loaf of bread, but anyway you haven't done it ... No, don't go away, sit down, sit down ... I criticize them because they're good enough that they could be better ... Why don't you paint one of their roosters in red and yellow? There are lots of roosters around here, all of them highly potent, stretching their necks every morning, crowing long before we get a new morning around *our* necks, ha ha. But you'd probably paint them in twilight too. I'm going to bed."

He waited a little but didn't ask. It was Victor who spoke. "Yes, I'll lock up. They can't get in."

When it was quiet Victor went out in the garden. The sky was as dark as the heath. Just at the edge of the horizon was a narrow yellow band of sunset. He waited, and then the lights of the train crept forth out of the night, a long way off. They called it the evening train, the one that never stopped. The local train came in just before dawn and paused for barely two minutes.

When the night came for his departure, Victor's papa was so tired that he barely turned in his bed and said, "Are you sure you have everything?" and fell back asleep.

The wind was blowing straight in from the grassy plain as usual. No lights had been lit yet in the henhouses. Victor put down his suitcase on the platform. It was very cold, the dark blue of the night had just begun to turn grey. You never knew, sometimes it came in early, and there had been times when the engineer simply drove right through.

Now the first rooster crowed. And he saw the train coming, a long row of lights. It stopped. It stopped out on the moor, quite a distance from the platform. He grabbed his suitcase and ran along the track, felt rather than saw the train start to move again. When he reached the first car, he jumped on but missed the second step and hit his chin on the iron railing, damn, wrestled his suitcase into the carriage, which was empty. And now the train stopped where it was supposed to stop, beside the platform. It just stood there, much longer than it should have. But you can never count on trains. The first light of dawn was reflected on the river, the bridge clearly outlined against it, along with someone on the bridge. The engineer did not blow the whistle as he started slowly forward and, just before the river slid past, Victor saw his papa throw up his arms in an extravagant gesture of farewell, and all the roosters crowed.

◆◆◆

At long last, Victor arrived at the large building where artists from every corner of the globe had their own studios for whatever period of time was considered appropriate to their talent – in Victor's case, seven weeks. The building was two blocks long and very tall. The lobby was huge, surrounded by glass walls. Outside, a stream of cars surged by in wave after wave. People who didn't seem to know one another sat around a glass table in black plastic armchairs, and, behind a counter, two young women were typing. Victor put his suitcase down beside the counter and waited. Between the onslaughts of traffic he could hear a strange whispering sound like rain but couldn't figure out where it came from. He lined up his documents on the counter, every paper signed, stamped and witnessed, everything in perfect order. Now the young woman approached. Victor gave her one additional paper, on which he had tried to express his gratitude and pride in this foreign language. She smiled a slightly

tired smile, he thought, and gave him a form to fill out.
Her face was small and tapered, with enormous eyes
painted black. She was dressed self-consciously in the
nonchalant offputting style which was that year's sexual
challenge. Victor thought her clothes indicated poverty.
He did not understand the form she'd given him – a lot
of text that maybe involved some sort of hasty commit-
ment. He covered the form with his hand and looked at
her. She pointed to the blank line at the bottom and he
signed his name. She gave him a key. The whispering
sound still filled the lobby like a distant waterfall without the slightest change in volume or quality. "What is
that sound?" he asked. And the young woman explained
something in detail that he didn't understand.

The lift was at the other end of the lobby. He walked to
it with all the others who were headed upstairs, a tightly
packed crowd. The lift rose quickly and soundlessly, no
one said a word but tried as best they could to avoid each
other's gaze. Now it came to his floor, the doors glided
open, he elbowed his way out, forgetting his suitcase, and
then the doors slid shut again. He pushed the button, all
the buttons at once, but the lift didn't return. He should
have hidden his money in a money belt, in a bag around
his neck, his passport, everything. It was terrible to have
come so far and then, the first day … He rushed up the
stairs to meet the lift, wait for it, then down to the lobby
again, where he shouted to the young woman with her
eyes outlined in black, "Suitcase! I am unhappy!"

She looked at him, shrugged her shoulders ever
so slightly in a gesture that he later realized was more

sympathetic than indifferent – and now the lift arrived, still jammed full of people. He dashed in, pushing his way heedlessly through the crowd, and grabbed his suitcase, which was still there, not gone. He opened the lid and found his money immediately. He was ashamed of himself. But no one seemed to notice him, they all went their own way and new people streamed into the lift and disappeared.

Victor was exhausted and felt a bit ill. He took his suitcase and climbed the stairs. There were long corridors running the whole length of the huge building, floor after floor, tunnels with distant openings of glass out towards the daylight. Doors at regular intervals, numbered black doors on both sides of the hallway. On the third floor, someone was playing the piano, the same passage over and over.

Victor found his way to Number 131, opened the door with the key the young woman had given him, then closed it behind him. He was home. It was very warm inside, and the sound of the distant waterfall was stronger than before. He stood still and stared at his studio, a large, anonymous square, light grey. Table, chair, bed – grey, black and brown – his own colours. The window was enormous, covered in plastic. And the whispering voice of falling water. Victor walked around the room listening until his hands felt the stream of warm air blowing up from the hot air registers under the window. He was hidden behind a drapery of hot whispering air, an invisible flood, inaccessible, as if at the ultimate edge of the world.

A little later someone came, a porter, and brought an easel. It was very large and looked like a doubled cross or a guillotine. Victor thanked him and pointed to the window, couldn't remember the word for "open" but the porter understood and made that little gesture with his shoulders, amiably apologetic. Afterwards, Victor rolled the easel in towards the wall. He thought the massive construction was far too obtrusive, intimidating in some vague way.

In the lobby they had a bulletin board with the names of all the residents, their native countries and room numbers. He had no compatriots. There was also a shelf with many small boxes for mail. His Papa had written.

Beloved son,
Writing a letter feels unusual, to say the least, and I assure you it won't be repeated often. Your change of scene is presumably quite powerful, which is excellent. Beware of advice and comfort and in any event forget what I said about red and yellow. Roosters are idiotic. Actually I have nothing special to say, in any case nothing I consider worthy of your attention – perhaps a hope that our new distance (geographic, that is) could give us surprising possibilities.

People have already started sending Christmas cards to each other, and their illustration choices are, if possible, even more banal than usual.
G.b.w.y. (God be with you)
Your father

One thing that bewildered Victor was that all the fortunate individuals allowed to work in this great building had nothing to do with one another. It was almost as if they avoided contact, in the lift, in the hallways. They scuttled through their doors as if the Devil himself were after them, and then the corridor was empty again. And yet they were all doing the same thing – a private idea that was more important than anything else, with only so much time to see it realized. Shouldn't they try to spend more time together? He wrote to Papa, a cautious letter. Papa answered immediately.

Beloved son,
You want to be left in peace and still be with others. It can't be done. Choose the one or the other, and whichever you choose you're up the creek. I know. The other night there was a wolf in my chair. Now don't imagine I'm nosy enough to ask how your work is going. For that matter, ignoring the expectations that always poison success is, in my opinion, an acceptable attitude. If you can afford it, you can always play around a bit with autonomy – if you know what I mean, said your papa …
G.b.w.y. and so forth

All the windows in the big building were covered with plastic – at least on the painter side, where an even northern light was considered essential – so no one could look out and see what was happening on the street. The rules also specified that each studio was reserved for one artist alone, the idea being that family or friends would break concentration.

Once a young man knocked on the door and came in and sat for a while. They had no common language, his guest did not want any refreshment, and from shyness and perhaps a kind of conceit Victor did not show him his work. The playful sign language that can be amusing in a café seemed suddenly inappropriate.

Victor knew that many of those whom the people behind the counter called inmates did not complete their months, their precious weeks, but swallowed their shame and fled back home to their own countries, unable to tolerate a life too luxurious, too warm, too lonely.

In the beginning, Victor worked in a state of ecstatic unreality. Early in the morning, long before the traffic began streaming endlessly past, the only window showing a light was his. The studio seemed as lovely to him as a geometric image of purity – the empty window, the absence of colour – an abstract space. The constant whispering and the torrent of warm air enclosed him day and night like a protective wall. From a need to complete the emptiness, he hid everything he'd brought from home in his suitcase under the bed. Sometimes he ate in a cheap café on a side street and he bought his art materials in a shop nearby. It never crossed his mind to venture deeper into the great foreign city. He had no need of it.

During this time of hectic happiness, Victor gave hardly a thought to his early youth. But there were certain simple objects that he missed and continually painted – a water jug, a brown platter ... He bought bread, potatoes, vegetables and set them out in his studio, but they remained alien, shadowless, meaningless. Then he painted the winter moor as he remembered it and knew it. No one and nothing bothered him. His works grew darker and darker and at last there was nothing but a narrow band of sunset yellow just above the horizon.

When Victor had three weeks left, he set out his paintings along the walls and looked at them. For a whole hour, he sat and just stared, surrounded by an unbroken moor, sometimes distant, sometimes closer. Occasionally there were people walking by in the snow, some with wagons, horses pulling loads, but mostly the landscape was empty, just a shade less uncaring without people and horses – and the constant table with the loaf of bread, the root vegetables, and the jug, all in a row as if in a shop, lit by a dead light, totally meaningless to him and to God and to the whole world!

Victor was gripped by a depression so bottomless that his whole body ached. He saw that he'd been a better painter before he left home. He threw himself on the bed and fell asleep.

It was almost evening when Victor awoke and remembered what had happened. The room was transformed, hostile, the noise of the hissing hot air seemingly an octave higher. He stuffed wet newspapers into the vents, but the cruel whispering continued. He tried to pry open the window with his knife, but it wouldn't give. Sobbing with rage, he fished out his dictionary to find the words he needed, ran down the stairs to the lobby, and knocked on the counter with his key, vehemently, shamelessly insisting on the young woman's attention. And when she came over with her little tapered face and her repellent clothing, he shouted, "Air! Hot air! I hate."

"Everyone does," she said quietly and gave him a form for complaints and a letter that had come with the evening post.

Victor ran out into the street and rushed head over heels into the foreign city. It was very cold. He walked at random, further and further, the streets grew steadily smaller and at every corner he chose the narrowest one. It was the hour just before dusk, all the shops still open, everyone buying and selling. He joined the stream of people sweeping along, flowing apart and together again. The pavement was slippery with discarded vegetables, the air reeked of food and humanity. Glittery Christmas decorations sparkled above the hawkers' stands along with sausages and animal carcasses adorned with gold and silver flowers, long strands of coloured lamps stretched across the street, above them the dark, crowded facades of the buildings, a canyon with the sky for a ceiling. The sunset had flared up into a penetrating blaze of red and pink roses, and for a short time the streets and houses were drenched in a fleeting embrace of unearthly sweetness, whereupon the heavens grew dark and sank down on the roofs.

Victor walked and wept but no one seemed to notice. The street altered with extraordinary speed. The shops were screeching down their blinds and turning out their lamps, the people were going home. In the end, only the cafés were lit and open. He went into one on a corner. There were only a couple of tables. A fire burned in a

stove at one end of the room; at the other end they'd
piled empty boxes and packing material against the wall.
Several men stood at the bar, talking together in low
voices. Victor got his coffee, moved further away, and
opened his letter.

Beloved son,
You may think that I don't know the great cities,
but I do, I knew them. They are splendid and
pitiless. Now you are there, G.b.w.y. Last night the
Wild Beasts went round our house, but don't let it
worry you in any way. I'm the only one who hears
them. No one has asked me to say hello and that's
probably a good thing. You might feel you have to
send them a postcard from the great city. Forgive
me, I don't actually feel contempt for anything. I
think of you sometimes, but I don't miss you more
than necessary.
Papa

PS One night there was a violent thunderstorm on
the heath. Imagine, in the middle of winter. You
should have been here. I got reckless, didn't close
the doors, and watched the way it rolled in and
burst into lightning and thunder and a downpour.
Just think of all the terrified roosters and hens. It
was lovely, washed clean!

PPS But the next night They were back again.
Don't worry about it. I just wanted to tell you

that They were back again. (They're not afraid of thunderstorms, ha ha.)

Victor went back to the café every evening when the streets were full of people. It wasn't as pretty as the first time, but the street was the same, swarming with movement, full of colours and smells and voices and all those faces.

They got to know him in the café. He already had his own table, a little round iron table behind the stove and a bit to one side. Every evening he drew faces on a big sketch pad, using only black. No one paid any attention. He drew the young woman with her eyes outlined in black and the faces in the corridors and the lift, finally the faces in the street. He captured them all in his despair and forced them to speak.

He went to the studio only to sleep, and he returned to the café every evening. Gradually his faces began to change, he could no longer control them, they just came, and he let them come and trapped them in an unreality that was entirely his own. He captured the invisible ones that roamed about the house where his papa lived, gave them horns and wings and crowns however he pleased, but hardest of all was to draw their eyes.

I punish them, he thought. I give them faces that they can't escape, they're imprisoned. They pursued me even when I was little. The wolf in Papa's chair! But all that matters is: these pictures are good.

One evening in the café, the proprietor came to Victor's table and said, "Here's a tramp who possibly

speaks the same language you do. He drinks only wine."
And he beckoned to an old man who was waiting by the
door.

Yes, the old fellow spoke the same language, but didn't
want to talk. He sat down as close to the stove as he could
and they drank hot red wine together. Victor showed
him his drawings. His guest looked at them closely but
said nothing. He declined Victor's invitation to spend
the night in his studio but thanked him solemnly, stood
up and, with a modest bow, left.

"Did you understand each other?" the proprietor
asked.

"Yes," Victor said. "We understood."

It had been a mistake to show his drawings. What
had he expected? Praise? Astonishment? Revulsion? Yes,
whatever, but not silence.

He didn't go back to the café. He continued working
in his room. He no longer called it his studio. His figures
grew larger, more unmanageable. They fought and made
love, they came close to suffocating from heat or loneli-
ness, perhaps from confusion, but he had no compassion.
He freed himself from them because it was necessary.
In the evenings, he went out into the city, wandered at
random without concern for anything and returned only
towards morning.

He sent the drawings to his father.

On his last day, he gave *Young Woman with Eyes
Outlined in Black* to its subject. She thanked him, a bit
surprised, and gave him a letter.

Beloved son,

They arrived. You have managed to portray my companions. You've given my other reality a face. Their hideousness calms me, there is no longer a wolf in my chair. And they're excellent.

But you might at least have sent them by registered mail. You never learn a thing about life's practical details. And of course you haven't given me an exact arrival date, but I go to the depot now and then, when it suits me.

Papa

The train stopped out on the moor, as inexplicably as before, and stood still for several minutes. It started moving again and Victor saw his father on the platform. They approached one another. Very slowly.

Premonitions

WHEN I WAS YOUNG, a remarkable woman lived in the village where I grew up. Her name was Frida Andersson. Frida lived alone in a cottage by herself but she had a daughter and a grandchild in the city. Sometimes in summer they would come to visit, but as Frida grew more and more peculiar, they began to stay away.

The trouble was, Frida was haunted by a bad conscience. It became an obsession that no one could help her with. No matter what went wrong in the village, she thought it was her fault. When the village misfortunes were insufficient, she began to concern herself with everything she read in the newspaper, and then, of course, her anxiety became endless. Everything was her fault. It got worse and worse. In the end she just sat on her steps and cried.

I realize that this may be hard to believe, but no matter how foolish Frida's misapprehensions became, they were a bitter reality for her. It was impossible to explain and convince, and severity had no effect at all. Now, years later, it occurs to me that perhaps we should have gone along with her delusions, but we didn't. When no one agreed with her, she found comfort and confirmation in superstitious signs. A mirror is broken, two knives are crossed – there are portents and omens everywhere, if only you're sufficiently open to them and to the guidance that comes from above.

You might suppose that Frida would have been an easy target for the village children, but it wasn't like that at all. They were fascinated. Every time something bad happened in the world, the children all ran to Frida to hear the ghastly details. She had a powerful imagination and she could tell a terrific story.

I really believe that the children helped her a great deal, perhaps more than her portents.

I was seventeen at that time and of course I knew how the world worked, and almost everything else, plus it goes without saying that I liked to contradict and argue. It's amazing that Frida liked me anyway.

On pleasant summer evenings we'd sit on her front steps and she'd tell me about what was going to happen. She'd warn me earnestly about the inevitable, the threat that comes steadily closer and eventually finds its catastrophe, which must always have a reason, a cause.

"And the cause, of course, is you," I said, being sarcastic.

"Naturally," Frida said and took my hand. "You know, on Friday morning a big white bird came and tapped its bill on the kitchen window three times. And what happened? There was an earthquake in California!"

I read intellectual books in those days and launched into an explanation of egocentricity, misdirected self-identification and God knows what else, and Frida looked at me in a friendly way and shook her head and said, "You'll learn. But it will take time."

I tried to brighten her up with the prospect of a summer visit by her daughter and granddaughter, but no, the child could fall in the well or drown in the marsh or get a fishbone caught in her throat and suffocate. Then I got tired and left.

That same summer, they were blasting for the new highway. It was a company from the city that was doing the work. They had a whistle they blew; then came the explosion. You got used to it.

The accident caused a sensation in the village. No one could understand why Frida couldn't stay home when the whistle sounded. If she didn't believe in the town's warnings she must nevertheless have had her own. There was no need for her to get hit in the head with a plain old piece of granite.

I went to the hospital and they said I could talk to her for only a couple of minutes. There wasn't a lot of her to see under all the bandages.

I held her hand and waited.

Finally she whispered, "What did I tell you? Now you have to believe me."

"Of course, Frida," I said. "You're going to be fine. Now you just rest and don't worry about a thing."

Then, her voice clear and distinct, Frida said, "Exactly. You know what? For the first time in my life, I'm not worried at all. It feels wonderful. And now I'm going to sleep for a while. See you later."

A whole mass of children were there for Frida's funeral. They seemed expectant. But nothing remarkable happened – except later that evening there was a thunderstorm.

Emmelina

WHEN OLD MISS SPINSTER on the third floor had uttered the last of her constant complaints and died peacefully in her sleep, many of her neighbours wondered what would become of the vast turn-of-the-century flat she had occupied for ninety years. Eventually they learned that it would go to Emmelina, nineteen, a kind of lady's companion who, for all anyone knew, had been plucked from an employment bureau and was, consequently, a completely unknown quantity. How the maid found out, no one knew. She certainly didn't get it from Emmelina, who never said a word about herself, or, for that matter, about much of anything.

In any case the will was hardly dictated by affection or gratitude. According to the maid, Old Miss Spinster might just as well have had a cat as her companion, and Emmelina's ministrations, though irreproachable, seemed to have been rendered somewhat absent-mindedly. Mostly she sat by the bed and read aloud until Old Miss Spinster grew angry with the book and wanted a new one, or just insisted on knowing how the story came out. If you're a maid, constantly taking things into or out of the room, you hear and see a great deal. Poor Old Miss Spinster had tried to knock some life into the exemplary Emmelina, make her good and mad, ring for her night and day to bring things she didn't need, complain to high heaven about this or that, but no, it's hard to upset a person like Emmelina, and there's something wrong with people who are always calm and quiet. It's not natural. "Almost a little creepy," the maid said, lowering her voice. "Sometimes that Emmelina sends shivers down my spine."

Now six months had passed and Emmelina was still living in the great flat. She changed nothing. Everything stayed the way it had been in Old Miss Spinster's days. She seemed to like the darkened rooms with their capricious and barely discernible collections of furniture and bric-a-brac. She could walk, or rather wander, from one room to the next, apparently quite content and without a thought for the future.

The maid, who continued to come once a week, could report that Emmelina slept in the dining room, the largest room in the flat by far, the chairs all lined up against the wall, and that she had a lot of crystal balls on the sideboard shelves, but if you're odd, you're odd, and that's all there is to it. Time passed and the neighbours forgot about Emmelina, who was seldom seen, and everything in the building returned to normal.

Later, it occurred to David, who lived on the floor below and worked in advertising, that he might have passed Emmelina on the stairs several times without noticing her, small and pale as she was. And then came that important evening.

The lamps had gone out in his flat. He couldn't find a torch and went out into the stairwell. And then he saw Emmelina coming down the stairs step by step with a candle in one hand. David studied her face, which was so calm, so absolutely tranquil, caressed by the evasive shadows of the candle flame. She struck him as ethereally and mysteriously beautiful.

That night, David called up an image of the girl with her candle to chase away the thing he feared, which was an insight that came back to him mercilessly every evening when it grew dark. The insight was that he hated his job but that he didn't have the courage to break out and begin again from the beginning. That may sound easy. Don't a lot of people turn their lives around at age thirty-five? No, they don't. They go on and on. They don't dare, they don't have the strength. They just can't bring themselves to make the break … Or maybe they think it won't make any difference.

The nights continued, and gradually the image of the girl with the candle faded. And after all, what did she have to do with his problem?

David had nightmares in which, jovial and unctuous, he tried to sign a client using the same amusing anecdotes over and over, repeating the same simplistic, popular slogans again and again to close the deal … Or he was on his way to an important business lunch and he'd forgotten the address, the client's name, the purpose of the meeting, and he was late, always late, running madly through the streets knowing he was betraying an important trust.

And then in the morning he'd go back to his office.

David wrote a letter to Emmelina and then tore it up.

And there was Knut. They got together now and then to have a beer and read the evening papers before going their separate ways. Knut had a job renting and selling cars a couple of blocks down the street. One time David was dangerously close to telling him about his despair but decided against it. He didn't need to watch Knut look down at his large hands in helpless concern, exactly the way he had always done at school whenever he was embarrassed.

At his job, Knut might sometimes say to a customer in passing, "As my good friend in advertising said about this model …" or "You might ask a friend of mine in the advertising business. He hangs out with a lot of corporate bigwigs who drive this car."

Now Knut finished his beer and folded his newspaper.

"I don't see so much of you these days," he said. "Lots of work?"

"You bet."

"Going well?"

"Sure," David said. "See you."

"So long," said Knut.

Of course he could approach someone else, the bartender at the Black Bear or the man at the newsstand, and pour out all his troubles recklessly and tell them that he really only wanted to die, and then of course it would be impossible ever to have another drink at the Black Bear or buy a paper at the corner.

In the end, David walked one flight up and rang Emmelina's bell, without knowing what he would say to her.

"Good evening," Emmelina said. "You live downstairs, don't you?" Coolly polite, completely at ease, she talked to him for a few minutes about nothing in particular. She did not ask why he'd come. The young woman struck him as intelligent, and David was grateful for that. He slept that night without dreaming.

They started going out in the evenings, always to the same restaurant on the next block. For David, these evenings became very important because of Emmelina's restful silence and her calm. She didn't seem to expect anything of him and appeared to be completely at peace with herself. She never said anything of significance, nothing personal, but what she did say was preceded by a little pause that left David in suspense – until the moment of expectation passed. He noticed that Emmelina took what he said almost literally, with a child's earnestness, and he decided never to burden her. It was enough just to be close to her, free from the others but still not alone.

David loved Emmelina's hair – straight, blonde, bobbed in front and shoulder-length on the sides, a sparkling head from which her face looked out as if from a window, a narrow face, not in any way remarkable except for her eyes, which were unusually light, almost colourless. And he liked the way she let her hair fall forward when she listened to him with her eyes cast down.

David tried to preserve her mysteriousness. He was protective of this fragile new friendship. But with all chivalric courtesy, he could still ascribe qualities to Emmelina, give her traits of character that she showed no trace of. He constructed a tender picture of her childhood and early youth, gave her little eccentricities, charming faults. It became a game that reality was not allowed to approach too closely.

And he thought, How does she see me? A tall man with glasses and a thin neck, conventionally well dressed ... Does she sense that I'm unhappy, does she realize how tightly I control myself? She asks no questions, ever ... Why not?!

One day Emmelina said, "I collect crystal balls. I'd like to show them to you."

On the way to Old Miss Spinster's flat, he said, "She was a pretty angry woman, the old lady. It must have been difficult for you at times."

"It wasn't a hardship. She needed to get angry. It calmed her."

"You read aloud to her, didn't you? People say she only wanted to know how the stories ended – but what if they ended badly?"

"I chose books that ended happily," said Emmelina. "So eventually she knew it would go well for her too."

"How do you mean?"

"But you already know that. She died in her sleep."

"You're a funny one," David said. "What would you read to me when the time came?"

"I'd read you the riot act," she said.

David laughed appreciatively. It was so rare these days that anyone could make him laugh and still keep an utterly straight face.

When David came into the gloomy, overcrowded flat, it frightened him. "But Emmelina," he said, "you can't live here!"

"It doesn't matter," she said. "And I may not stay very long."

The crystal balls were very beautiful, some of them transparent, others filled with mist.

"Good hobby," David said and smiled at her. "What do you see in them? Something you wish for? Do you get a glimpse of the future?"

"No," said Emmelina. "They're empty, which is why I can stare into them practically forever."

David was concerned. It seemed to him that Emmelina needed to see people more. He would introduce her to his friends, first of all to Inger and Ines.

They received Emmelina with an easy friendliness but came gradually to see her as a lovable curiosity, worthy of acceptance and protection but not really of being taken seriously. They did not shorten her name but continued to call her Emmelina, the name itself an archaic pleasantry worthy of preservation. But mostly they called her "My Dear".

Sometimes they talked right past Emmelina, as if she weren't even there, but they meant no offence. Yet sometimes when she spoke everyone went silent and listened attentively, almost expectantly. When whatever Emmelina had to say struck them as banal, however, the conversation would continue without her, almost with a sense of relief.

"She's sweet and pleasant, of course," Inger said, "but isn't she a little naïve? And what about her sense of humour?"

Inger was a large, pretty woman who kept close track of everyone she'd slept with over the years and couldn't help bossing them around and seeing to it that they behaved themselves as well as could be expected. One day she asked David how he was, if he was feeling better. And he recalled with sharp self-loathing the time he'd gone to Inger and told her of all his misery with his job and even wept in her arms.

Now her question made him belligerent. "How do you mean?" he said. "Why wouldn't I be feeling all right?"

"Darling," she said, "I know you're terribly proud. But promise me not to brood about all those things any more? All right? Good. That makes me feel much better."

He had allowed her to get really close, and she'd become painfully tactful, conspiratorial even, now that she was in possession of his weakness. And he couldn't even dislike her because she was so clearly and completely kind.

At his job, things did not improve. David was late for appointments, barely polite to clients, and an ironic tone crept into his popular slogans that discredited what he was trying to sell.

"What's troubling you?" his boss asked in a friendly way, because he liked David.

And all at once David understood that he was, as Knut would have put it, doing everything he could think of to get himself fired. But cowardice took a new grip on him and he promised to pull himself together and try harder.

One day as David and Emmelina were sitting at their usual table at the restaurant, he gave her a present, a glass ball. If you shook the ball, a snowstorm whirled up and gradually fell on a little Swiss chalet with tinfoil windows.

"Do you like it?" he asked.

Emmelina smiled and touched his hand, a friendly gesture, but not unlike the appreciation one shows for the clumsy gift of a child.

David was silent for the rest of the meal and she didn't ask him why he didn't eat.

Finally he burst out, "You don't care about anything!"

Emmelina stared at him. She waited.

He went on. "Emmelina, what do you mean to do with your life, your only life? You can't just let time go by!"

"But my life is good," Emmelina said.

"No, it's not! A flower trying to grow in a cellar! Is there nothing you really care about, nothing you long to do? To achieve something, create something, maybe with your own hands? Discover new ideas that are bigger and more important than yourself? Do you understand?"

"Yes," Emmelina said.

"Listen to me. If, right now, you could get your wish, like in the fairy tale, you know, you can wish for anything at all but only one wish, what would you wish for? You can sing more beautifully than anyone else in the world, or know everything about the stars, or know how to make a clock or build a boat. Anything at all!"

"I don't know," said Emmelina. "What about you?"

"Come on, let's go," said David curtly. "I can't breathe in here."

They walked up the street, past Knut's garage, which was closed for the day, and on to the park. A light rain was falling, very light. As they walked under the trees, David talked about his agony at work, he poured out the whole miserable story – but in the third person. When he was done, Emmelina said, "I feel sorry for him. But if he's too weak to live, wouldn't it be better if he didn't?"

That frightened David.

One evening when David and Emmelina were at Ines's place, there was an awkward incident. After dinner, Ines was telling them about her new party dress. "Wait a minute," she said. "I'll put it on. And you have to tell me what you really think!"

They waited. Ines came in.

Emmelina said, "It's very pretty." And added, as if parenthetically, "But it doesn't suit you."

Afterwards, down on the street, David said he thought she shouldn't have said that. "Couldn't you lie a little just to be nice?"

"Of course I could. But not yet."

"I don't understand you," David said. "But you could try to be nice to my friends."

Things were even worse at Inger's. She had a large cage of canaries. One of them, plucked naked and miserable, was being chased around the cage by the other birds, and Inger said, "What should I do with the poor thing?"

"Kill it," said Emmelina.

"But I just can't! Maybe the feathers will grow out again ..."

"They'll never get the chance," Emmelina said. She opened the cage, caught the bird quick as a wink and broke its neck. She laid the pathetic little carcass on the table.

Thank you," said Inger uncertainly, taking a tiny step back. But David saw, and he saw the look in Inger's eyes, and he said, "I think we should go home."

One day, David took Emmelina to see Knut. "Emmelina," he said, "remember that Knut is my friend."

They walked to the garage and Knut showed her the best cars he had. David was amazed to hear her ask very knowledgeable questions. She seemed to know a great deal about cars. Knut was enthusiastic. He talked at length about catalytic converters and overhead camshafts, told his guest about all the latest fine points, as he called them, and she seemed to understand everything he said.

"But do you even know how to drive?" said David on their way home. "How do you know all that stuff? Or are you just pretending again?" And before she had time to say nothing at all in reply, he said, "Forget it. Knut liked you."

Now the snow melted and blue patches opened in the sky. The air was mild. David decided to borrow the company car and drive out to the country somewhere with Emmelina. She needs it, he thought. We'll take a picnic lunch and spend the whole day outdoors. But Emmelina said she was busy over the weekend. David didn't ask, but he was bewildered and a little hurt. Every time he'd called, she'd been at home and had no plans, was never in a hurry but simply there. He'd come to count on it.

♦♦♦

Old People's Homes – those large buildings in out-of-the-way places outside the city – are all much alike. At visiting time, the buses seldom stop, just slow down a bit and then drive on.

The receptionist recognized her. One nurse stopped in the corridor and said to another, "Here she is again. You'll see, another one of them will go. Last time it was Room 25. Keep an eye on her."

"I don't believe all that. She's just an ordinary bleeding heart with time on her hands."

"No, no, she always knows when one of them's going to kick off. Are they afraid of her?"

"Not a bit. If anything, she calms them. Now don't be childish. One of them thinks he's Napoleon and there's another thinks she's the Queen of Sheba. So why can't that girl imagine she's death's little helper?"

And they walked off in opposite directions.

♦♦♦

"Your little friend," Ines said, "who's she playing at? Mystery girl? The little truth teller? Honestly, David, there's something there I don't like. What's her game? We don't know."

"So what?" David said. "Leave her alone. Why do you have to know what her game is, if she even has one? You usually just let people be themselves, a very nice quality."

Ines shrugged her shoulders. "You don't understand," she said. "As far as I'm concerned, people can be as odd as they like, that's up to them. But this girl is odd in the wrong way. She's sort of not really of this world, if you know what I mean."

No," David said rather stiffly. "I really don't. Let's talk about something else."

"Fine, fine, whatever you say. But all the same, take care. There's something about her – I'm sorry, I can't help it – that's a little frightening."

They were trying to distort his picture of Emmelina, each in her own way. It was better to see them without her. Or maybe not see anyone but Knut.

They were sitting reading their newspapers at their usual place. Knut would get up now and then and put a couple of coins in the slot machine, but he never won, so he'd come back to the table.

"You know what?" he said. "I had such a funny dream last night, although I don't usually dream at all. What it was was that we were working together at the garage. You were great at selling cars, talked people practically to pieces, you know, like you do at your job. And they said we could start serving beer. Weird, huh?"

"Very," said David. "Sounds nice. Knut? About women. I don't understand them. They're strange."

Knut thought for a moment, then said, "How much do you like her?"

"I don't know."

"Have you asked her?"

"No."

"And now you don't know what to do next?" Knut leaned across the table and said, "Maybe I'm wrong, but couldn't you try to impress her? Tell her about your plans for the future, get her interested, then you'll be planning together and that will make the whole thing easier, right? Does she know what you want, what your goals are?"

"I suppose she does," said David heavily. "She seems to know everything, and that's why there's nothing for me to say. You see?"

"No, not really," Knut said and stared at his hands. And then they talked about other things.

Spring had now finally come in earnest. David had once heard or read that spring can be dangerous for people with dark thoughts, a risky crater in the annual cycle, roughly similar to four o'clock in the morning – the easiest time to let go. David made no attempt to curb these thoughts. On the contrary, he dove headlong into them in defiance of all the encouragement offered him on every side – sympathy, advice, concerned questions, his overly friendly and embarrassed boss at work, and Inger, inescapable, more maternal than ever – everyone trying to help except Emmelina. She was silent, the only one capable of understanding.

He was feeling terrifically sorry for himself. He put his troubles all in a row and scrutinized them with bitter satisfaction. Staying in his present job – out of the question.

Starting over with something he couldn't handle and cared nothing about – out of the question. Everything else – out of the question. Absolutely. He was punishing Them, It, The Others, Whatever, by not shaving, not making his bed, not doing his laundry, buying canned food he didn't even like and eating it directly from the container – yes, there were lots of ways to demonstrate a desperate man's contempt.

And, most all, he played with the notion of his own death.

Early one Monday morning, Emmelina appeared outside David's door. Very calmly she told him that he had to quit his job.

"It's important," she said. "Don't wait till tomorrow, David, I beg you."

"What are you talking about?" David said.

"You know perfectly well what I'm talking about."

"Emmelina, you don't understand."

"Yes, I do, believe me." And without giving him time to reply she turned and walked up the stairs.

That evening, David went to her and said, "I couldn't do it."

"I knew it," she said. "You were scared."

"What do you know about scared?" he shouted. "Everyone gets scared! You and your damned crystal balls, empty, stupid crystal balls!" And he slammed the door and went home.

The next morning, David called his office and said he was sick. In fact, he thought, in a way I've never been as sick as I am now because I might just as well die. I'm ready to go, even though it doesn't show. To be on the safe side, he took aspirin and checked his temperature, which was normal, went back to bed and pulled the quilt over his head but didn't disconnect the telephone. It didn't ring until early evening, and then it was only Inger.

"My dear," she said, "are you sick? Is it your throat? No? How are you feeling?"

"Awful," David said. "This could last a long time."

"Can I come up and make you some tea or something? Maybe we should get a doctor to come have a look at you."

"No, no, it's nothing, nothing at all! I just want to sleep and be left in peace, absolutely in peace. Do you understand?"

Before David could repair his rudeness, Inger asked if he wanted her to call Emmelina.

He hadn't expected that of Inger. For a moment, his voice failed him.

"Are you there?" she said.

"Yes. Good. Good idea. Inger. Thanks. You'll tell her that I'm feeling really bad?"

David waited, but the doorbell didn't ring. It was the telephone that rang, and it was Emmelina, finally. "David? Inger said you were sick. She was very friendly."

"She was? Why wouldn't she be?"

"She doesn't like me," Emmelina explained, almost parenthetically. "What's wrong with you?"

"I don't know. Everything's wrong."

"Of course it's wrong. But I think you'd better get up. I'll wait down at the corner."

For a moment, anger flooded through him again, but all he said was, "You have to remember that I'm very weak."

"I know that," Emmelina said.

Outdoors, the spring dusk was almost warm.

She said, "Let's go and see Knut. He's unhappy that he sees so little of you."

"Have you spoken to him?"

"No. But he's unhappy."

Knut stood up when they appeared. "Hi," he said. "How nice. Miss, two large beers and a small Madeira for the lady. Busy at work?"

"Fairly busy … How about you? Have you sold anything lately?"

"Yes, indeed. A Mercedes. Used. I got the sale by telling the buyer you had a friend who owned the same model. I should almost give you a commission! And what are you two up to this evening?"

"Nothing much."

"Good. Everyone needs to take some time to just be. It's restful. And right and proper. Like little Emmelina here, she's just herself, she just is. Right?" He smiled at her and then went off to put some coins in the slot machine.

They stayed quite a while and talked only when they had something to say.

When David and Emmelina walked home, it had started to rain.

"Spring rain is wonderful," David said. "Really. It makes all the colours stronger."

David didn't know which was greater, his affection for Emmelina or his respect. Plus somewhere there was a little fear, the kind you feel for things that are alien and different, unpredictable. He was unable to hold on to the image of the girl with the candle. The unreachable had somehow grown even more distant.

Then came a time when the maid answered Emmelina's telephone. No, the young lady was not in, no, she had left no message. Every day the same thing, no matter what time of day. She just wasn't there. David didn't let himself worry. It didn't occur to him that something could have happened to her. He was just immeasurably hurt at being left in the lurch just when he needed her most.

And when she finally came, he shouted at her. "Where have you been? You're not my friend! You know what I'm going through – and this is the way you behave!"

"I've been busy," she said. "But now I'm here." She walked past him into the room and sat down at the table. David looked at her beautiful hair, heavy and shimmering. "I'm so terribly tired," he said. "You know that."

Emmelina said, "David, I can't wait for you any longer. It's getting late for me and I have to go."

"You sound so strict," he said. "Why are you being that way?"

"Sleep a little," Emmelina said. "I'll be here when you wake up."

He had recurrent dreams. How he would do it, cleverly contrived so that no one would have a bad conscience – and then right away came the other dream, where he did it with morbid clarity and left everyone in unforgiving self-reproach.

Emmelina was there when he awoke. She was no longer strict but asked him tenderly, "David, do you think it's worth it? Think about it. Aren't you the least bit curious?"

David wasn't listening. "Emmelina!" he burst out. "Do you know that I love you?" And he added quickly, "Don't say it. Don't say you knew it."

She let her lovely hair fall forward so he couldn't see her face as she answered. "I didn't know."

Afterwards, when she'd gone, all he could remember was that she'd promised to come back, but later – "much later" is what she'd said.

David slept all night without dreaming and woke up sometime in the middle of the day and knew it was not too late for anything any more, not for anything whatever. By and by he took the bus to work and talked to his boss. "Good," his boss said. "I understand. Good luck, and let me know how you're doing."

It all went very smoothly. David waited a couple of days in order to have his new freedom all to himself, then he walked upstairs and rang Emmelina's bell.

It was the maid who opened the door. "No," she said, "the young lady has moved, crystal balls and all. I'm on my way as well. Nice weather we're having, don't you think?"

"Yes indeed," David said. "And she left no new address?"

"No, she didn't. I'm very sorry."

"Don't be," David said. "She promised to come back."

My Friend Karin

1

MY MOTHER AND I CAME TO SWEDEN to visit Grandpa and Grandma in their big parsonage in a valley by the sea. The house is full of uncles and aunts and cousins.

Karin is seven months older than me and also pretty. She comes from Germany. I love her.

One day we built a throne for God on the hayfield, and that's what I'd like to tell about. When God's throne was finished, we decorated it with daisies and danced around Him. It was Karin's idea.

And then something dreadful happened. I don't know what came over me, but suddenly I ran up to the throne and sat down on it. Karin stopped dancing. She was horrified, and so was I. I think we expected to be struck by lightning.

I didn't have the nerve to sit there more than a few seconds, but I took the opportunity to imagine what it would feel like to be omnipotent. But I didn't really have enough time.

That was yesterday. Karin said only one thing. She said, "I forgive you." And now she doesn't want to talk to me any more. She is a good friend of God's, which I've heard about quite often enough. She doesn't talk that much about Jesus, although he could do just as many miracles as God.

There's a thing I've been thinking about, namely Jesus and Judas. Jesus knew perfectly well that Judas was going to betray him. It was settled ahead of time what Judas would do, and he couldn't do otherwise because it was God's plan. And it was decided that Judas would go hang himself afterwards and become the world's biggest scoundrel. Okay, so here's my question: Is that fair? And then, after all his horror and his terrible remorse, Judas was probably forgiven anyway, because God and Jesus always forgive anyone who repents at the last minute.

Uncle Olov said once that they have a copyright on forgiveness, and what he meant was that you can't take anyone else's forgiveness seriously. He said to Mama once, "All that stuff about letting people be born in sin and giving them a bad conscience and then nobly forgiving them. What kind of nonsense is that?"

But Uncle Olov doesn't believe in God, which is a terrible thing. Otherwise he's very nice.

I've been wondering. The person who forgives is always superior, and the person who gets forgiven feels wretched. I don't know who to forgive so I can be the superior person. What Uncle Olov said about God giving us a bad conscience is absolutely true. I mean, whatever you do it's just as bad, right from the start, because we're born in sin and have to pray for forgiveness all the time. I think it gets kind of boring.

But now I want to tell something nice. It was when I found Grandma's book about missionaries converting the heathens. Grandma's other books weren't much fun, but this one was really good. You know, some heathens worshiped the sun and others believed in someone named Pan, and he just went around in the woods and played the flute and didn't take anything seriously. Then they had a totem pole and all sorts of stuff but they completely believed in all of it until they were converted. It was a good book. I read it at night after Karin had gone to sleep, all that time she wouldn't speak to me. During the day I read the *Five Books of Moses* out in the meadow. That was even more exciting and also better written. Among other things, I found it comforting to see that God could behave badly. His feelings were often hurt and He could be jealous of other gods, and He took the time and trouble to wreak quite a lot of vengeance. Of course, that did not diminish my respect for Him, but I did start taking morning prayers and Bible studies a little less seriously, and that was too bad. I mean, not *bad*, but it was a shame, if you know what I mean.

2

That was the summer Grandpa was working on his great dissertation and needed to concentrate. Since he knew how much Karin's papa Hugo liked to preach, he let him take over the daily text and say grace before meals, but Uncle Hugo was so zealous that he also took over much of the Bible study and a lot of the hymn singing. All the relatives had to attend. He looked closely and knew exactly who was missing. Although he gave up on Uncle Olov right from the start.

Uncle Hugo had a brown velvet coat and a white cap with a peak and he played the cello.

Sometimes I wondered what God must think of Uncle Hugo, who in a way had stolen all the glory. After all, my grandfather was the Royal Chaplain, and Uncle Hugo was just an ordinary priest who'd married his daughter. But he carried on as if we were facing the Day of Judgment and he knew best. Although he was really nice and very worried about all of us.

More than anything, Uncle Hugo loved his cello. It was brown and shiny as a chestnut. It cracked once, and he was beside himself. And the only one who could mend it was Uncle Olov, who was good at anything that had to do with wood. But the sad part was that of all Grandpa and Grandma's children, it was only Uncle Olov who didn't believe in God. The other uncles could make a lot of noise about how they didn't believe in God, but they carried on so dreadfully that it seemed to me that deep down they really did believe after all.

But Uncle Olov just said nothing and looked embarrassed and went out to his woodworking shed. I don't think it was easy for Uncle Hugo to take his cello out to the shed. But Uncle Olov fixed it perfectly and it was just as beautiful as ever.

One time Mama was really mad after morning prayers. Uncle Hugo had prayed for all of us as usual and given thanks for everything we'd been given in our spiritual lives – and then he went and gave thanks for everything Mama had been given in her material life!

I said to Karin, "Your papa doesn't know a bloody thing about my mama!"

She just looked at me with her beautiful eyes and smiled as if she was forgiving me for saying something really stupid.

I admired Karin, enormously. When she sang harmony in the hymns, you just shivered with divine joy and sadness. She was like a bird from heaven above all the others, but she was afraid of wasps. One day a wasp came in during morning worship at breakfast and flew around her and Karin stopped singing and just went berserk. We were hearing about Job's Afflictions that day, I remember. That wasp wasn't the least bit interested in attacking Karin, he just wanted to find his way out, but she leaped up and started flailing her arms and screaming and spoiled the whole atmosphere completely. When the cousins saw Karin carrying on that way, they all started screaming themselves, and I started laughing so hard I was crying and had to leave the table. It still makes me laugh to think about it.

One day just when the sun was going down, Uncle Hugo took my hand and said we should take a walk in the meadow. In the middle of the meadow, under Grandpa's huge birch tree that he planted a hundred years ago, we sat down in the grass and Uncle Hugo said, "How wonderfully peaceful. I'd like to have a little talk with you." First he talked about Grace and then he started talking about Satan and said he was very sad for my sake. I had not understood that Satan's minions were everywhere – a single wicked thought could bring them closer. "Closer and closer," Uncle Hugo said. "In the evening before you go to sleep, they're all around you, although you can't see them. The only thing you can do then is pray. I would very much like to help you. Will you talk to me about these things?"

But I didn't know what to say about them.

When evening came, I got under the quilt and told the minions, "Go away! Go away!"

Uncle Hugo was right. They really were everywhere.

3

Many years later I got to make my first trip abroad and stay with the Uncle Hugo and Aunt Elsa in Germany. Karin had grown even prettier and still more serious. Suddenly we had difficulty talking to each other, and I could see that made Aunt Elsa unhappy.

They lived in a very small city in the Rhine Valley. The city was surrounded by broad fields and meadows with groves of acacia here and there. A small, narrow, brown river wandered off toward the horizon. Every day we went to hear Uncle Hugo preach in the church hall, and it was always full. One time after his sermon he said that now we were going to pray for a dear guest who had come from a foreign country. "She has not been granted the grace of atonement. Let us pray for her." And everyone bowed their heads in prayer and then looked at me. Afterwards I went to Aunt Elsa, and she said, "Don't take it so seriously. He means well. He has so much love to give."

So as not to make them unhappy, I would take long walks out of town when I wanted to smoke. Members of the congregation might have seen me otherwise and told people what I'd done. As I sat in the shade of an acacia's delicate foliage, I could see that the landscape, in all its horizontal dreariness, was nevertheless beautiful, and I thought about Uncle Hugo, what an unusually virtuous person he was and how he was only trying to help people live slightly purer lives in accordance with God's intentions. That is, if any human being can venture to say what God's intentions are.

When I got back, I stopped in the doorway and burst out, "How nice it smells here – just like home!"

Aunt Elsa said, "It's denatured alcohol. We're washing windows."

Just outside the town there was a very pretty little park-like wood. The trees were tall and old. Uncle Hugo and I walked there once through a greenish dusk shot through with shafts of sunlight. He was wearing his brown velvet coat and his white peaked cap.

"I love this wood," he said. "It makes me feel so peaceful. It's called Buchenwald, beech wood. I always come here when I'm having trouble with a sermon." After a while, he went on. "My parishioners believe in me. But sometimes they come and ask why God couldn't prevent some great misfortune or injustice. 'It would be so easy for Him,' they say."

"And what do you tell them? That God's ways are inscrutable?"

"More or less," said Uncle Hugo sadly. "It isn't always so easy."

Sometimes we talked in his garden right behind the house. It was really a wonder. Small as it was, it had everything that great patience and a love of flowers could achieve.

"I learned from your grandfather," he said. "Or maybe even more from the Japanese. You have to plan. You have to replace plants that have stopped blooming with the ones that are about to start, and colours are very important. You can't have colours that don't go together blossoming at the same time."

"But they do," I said. "Think of a meadow. Everything haphazard."

And Uncle Hugo explained that we're not to compete with God's garden, where miracles occur, but if we indulge the whims of nature for even a moment, the harvest will be mostly weeds.

Uncle Hugo had one theme he often returned to, and that was the wise and the foolish virgins. And, one day as we were weeding the garden, he asked me if I could paint a picture of them for him, preferably together with Christ.

The picture grew very large and was very difficult to paint. Uncle Hugo came and looked at it now and then and said the virgins were going to be very fine and beautiful but "I don't recognize Christ."

I had thought to make Christ less gentle than he's usually portrayed and capture some of his critical strength, the controlled violence I've always expected of him –but it didn't turn out right. I moved him further and further away until he was almost nothing but a bright shape in the distance. I'd rubbed his face so hard and so often that it was all just rough and blurry.

Uncle Hugo shook his head and said, "I can see that you're moving further and further from Jesus. You're no Gotteskind, and if you're not a friend of Christ's, then you can't paint His picture. But we'll hang it up anyway."

Karin's room was a girl's room all in white, surely unchanged from when she was little. Our beds stood against opposite walls and between them was a window with white curtains. You could see right out over Uncle Hugo's garden. Somehow Karin didn't fit in, although it was her room – something about her earnestness, her restless eyes. She read the Bible every night before going to sleep. One night she asked me if I believed in the absolute.

"How do you mean?" I said.

"To believe in one thing absolutely, the only path to salvation, giving up everything that might stand in your way. Everything."

I didn't know what to answer.

She came over and put her gold bracelet in my hand. "It was Grandma's," she said. "I like it too much and therefore I have to give it up. Believe me, I do it with joy, I'm relieved." She looked at me with a kind of strict tenderness. Then she went back to her reading.

Aunt Elsa was disappointed in us. Maybe she thought friendship between us would liven up her long letters to a beloved sister.

One day Aunt Elsa wanted me to go out for a walk with her, since it was such a beautiful day. She set off straight across the meadows, full of wild poppies. There was no breeze. It was hot. Aunt Elsa was wearing her dark glasses. She said nothing.

Only when we had left the town far behind did she ask me if I'd ever heard of secret microphones, listening devices. I answered that I'd heard of them, but surely there weren't any such things in an ordinary parsonage?

She laughed at me and said, "He doesn't believe in them. He won't believe anything bad about his country. But the devil's minions are everywhere."

Aunt Elsa talked for a long time. It was like she was going to burst. Finally she said, "Give my love to my sister. Try to tell her all the things I don't dare write to her. Now I have to get home to make lunch. Hugo eats far too little. He wears himself out with parish work."

"But doesn't he understand what's happening?" I asked.

Aunt Elsa didn't answer. It was way too hot, and I wasn't yet accustomed to unhappy people. But it occurred to me that she needed to protect Uncle Hugo.

Among other things, from her homesickness. And from becoming aware of the perilous borderlands of religion, which he was incapable of understanding.

Finally she said, "Have you talked to Karin? I mean do you two talk to each other? Do you understand each other?"

"Yes. Absolutely. I love her."

"Is she happy? Is she calm?"

"Yes," I said. "Utterly. Completely calm."

The last night of my stay at the parsonage, Aunt Elsa came up to our room and put a bottle of red wine on the table. "Don't tell him," she said. "He wouldn't understand." Then she smiled and went back downstairs.

"How nice of her," Karin said. "She wants us to enjoy ourselves." Karin filled our glasses. "You don't know," she went on. "You don't know. It comes like a waterfall, like music, you're very close to the absolute and then it vanishes again. Mama doesn't know, no one knows. All material things become superfluous, and you're afraid."

I asked cautiously, "But what are you planning to do with your life?"

Karin looked past me and said, "It's a matter of loving, absolutely. First and foremost, God. And then your neighbour, your enemies, the smallest sparrow and blade of grass. Therefore", she added, "I can't afford and I don't have time to love those who expect me to love them. I'm forced to give them up."

"But who is your neighbour?" I said. "We're just ordinary people, after all. We like you, I mean, your family, your friends, your best friend."

Karin smiled and explained. "You don't understand. I can honour them, I can honour you. You're a gift that I'm grateful for, but not something to keep for myself."

I didn't understand, not then. I admired Karin as much as ever, but my feelings were confused.

The next morning, I went with Uncle Hugo and Aunt Elsa on his vacation to Switzerland, to Grindelwald, which they loved. From there I would travel on to Finland. Karin stayed at home. She stood on the steps and watched us leave, as serious as ever.

Grindelwald – that frightening landscape of craggy perils and fabricated idylls where the shadows come too early and there is no horizon …

We hiked off in a large group, higher and higher amidst the beauty of the wildflowers. Uncle Hugo had his alpenstock and his camera. He stopped often to take pictures, he changed his film, he took small detours – and suddenly he was gone. They searched for him, had worried discussions, time passed. Aunt Elsa sat on a rock, silent, unmoving, conveying her anxiety right through her dark glasses. I could see how much she loved Uncle Hugo.

When they finally found him, he was not even embarrassed, just happy as usual, and he smiled at everyone with his unnaturally white teeth. "A little adventure!" he said. "Now let us walk on through this glorious, open-hearted world."

We came to a little Alpine tarn. It mirrored the sky and lay like a little blue jewel among those dreadful crags. Aunt Elsa turned to me and finally spoke. "You know, that little tarn is so like him. That's his very nature. Pure."

On my very first trip I had made a vow – I would swim in every new body of water I came to, a river, a sea, a lake. But Alpine tarns are really a little too cold.

4

Many years passed once again, and then after the war Karin came to stay with me. She met my friends and everyone liked her. They were fascinated. "Are you really related?" they said. "She's simply wonderful, and so calm and collected!"

Karin said very little. They didn't realize they'd been introduced to a saint.

I now loved Karin without envy. I wanted to give her presents, anything she might need or want, but each time she had to go into the bathroom first and talk to God to see if she could accept the gift. There were some things she decided she could keep, but most of it had to be thrown into the sea. The things Karin liked most were quite literally thrown into the sea.

I asked about Uncle Hugo and Aunt Elsa, and Karin replied that she had given them up because she loved them too much. "I will give you up as well," she said.

And then I knew that she loved me, but it was a sad kind of joy.

Electronic music had just begun to appear at that time – Pierre Schaeffer, Klaus Schulze – an abstract music of galactic desolation that enraptured me. I wanted Karin to hear it too, but I should never have played that record. I explained that this was a new thing they were experimenting with. "Now just listen to this," I said. "It's like the pulsing of the spheres in space. Don't you think?"

"Quiet," said Karin. "I'm listening."

We listened together. The room seemed to throb electronically. Karin had gone pale and sat utterly motionless.

I jumped up to turn off the music but Karin yelled, "Don't! This is important to me!"

I should have remembered this was the moment when Dante descended into the Underworld and was met by the cries of the lost souls.

"I know," Karin said. "This is it. Now comes the voice of God."

And it came. How could she have known!? A deep, sorrowful bass that cut through the music with incomprehensible words and vanished into the galaxy amidst the vibrations that finally lost themselves in silence.

"Forgive me …" I said. "You understand, this is a new kind of music they've just invented."

"No," said Karin calmly, "it has always existed. The lost souls are with us always, I know them. It's like a grey wave – any time, any place, on the street, on the train – obliterating everything. They cry for help and we sink in sin, theirs and our own. Can you play it again?"

But I didn't want to.

When I hugged her, she held me the way you protect and comfort a stranger who has injured or made a fool of himself.

When Karin had gone, the bathroom continued to be a sacred place for quite some time. Now and then I would go there to seek answers to the unanswerable questions.

A Trip to the Riviera

WHEN MAMA'S SIXTIETH BIRTHDAY approached, she made it known that gifts were unnecessary but that she did have one simple wish – to visit Barcelona in an effort to understand Gaudí's architecture. She also wanted to visit the Riviera, specifically, Juan les Pins. And of course she wanted her daughter Lydia to come with her, since they were used to living together. But the journey must not cost too much.

Everyone explained that the Riviera was very expensive, but a dream is a dream and when dreams grow old, they grow strong.

The travel bureau reported that, unfortunately, they knew of no cheap hotels on the Riviera, in any case not in the vicinity of Juan les Pins, not even pre-season.

Friends and acquaintances made some calls. Mama's ideas always amused them. And finally someone's cousin came up with the address of a *pension* that was cheap if you were careful not to come during the season. It was owned by a certain Monsieur Bonel.

"Lydia," said Mama, "write that we're interested but we want only one meal a day." She had calculated that if they travelled third class and spent only one day in Barcelona and avoided all unnecessary expenses, they could manage well enough.

"Of course, Mama," said Lydia and started looking for someone to cover for her at the library.

They began their trip by boat. Their friends stood on the quay and waved. Up on deck, Mama was clearly visible with her white hair and her large, light grey hat, broad-brimmed, strict, with a low crown – the very epitome of hatness. She hadn't changed her headgear since 1912.

Everyone cheered and the boat pulled away.

At long last, Mama and her daughter arrived in Barcelona, where she spent the entire day admiring Gaudí.

"Lydia," she said, "I don't know a thing about architecture, but here we see the irrational in all its violent, headstrong glory. That's sufficient. I don't need to understand. By the way, I think I'll buy a new hat, a toreador hat."

It wasn't easy to find the right size for her majestic topknot, but the hat was found and purchased, and now Mama was tired and wanted to sit down and have a cup of coffee. They went into a little café with only a couple of tables and a counter. The walls were decorated with bullfight posters. A number of older men stood talking at the bar. When Mama entered in her toreador hat, they turned and looked at her and the hat and expressed their appreciation in a quiet and respectful "Olé". Someone set out a chair, but she preferred to stand. Each of the ladies was served a small glass of sherry. The café had gone quiet. Now one of the old men came up to Mama and lowered himself on one knee. She handed him her shawl.

Whereupon, his gaze fixed on hers, he performed the Bullfight, the ritual movements that precede and culminate in the death of the bull. His friends stood motionless in rapt attention, sometimes uttering a barely audible "Olé". When the bull had been dispatched, Mama emptied her glass, thanked them all with a quick bow and someone opened the door.

"That was elegant." Lydia said. "Where did you get the idea for the shawl? If only Papa could have seen it!"

"Dear child," Mama said, "he probably would have wanted to stay so he could get to know everyone. He never understood showmanship. Moreover, your father always used to spoil our travels with homesickness." She added, "Sherry is a ghastly drink."

After their adventure in Barcelona, the trip continued to Juan les Pins, where the travellers took a taxi to Monsieur Bonel's *pension*. The *pension* was very small, and it was not by the sea. Monsieur Bonel came towards them in his long green apron, glanced at the taxi meter, and said, "No tip. He has cheated you." Then he took care of their luggage and treated his guests to a small glass of sherry in the lobby, a formal and rather dreary room kept in deep shade by several potted palms. He asked them about their journey and then fell silent. Finally, with great effort, he said, "Mesdames, I am devastated. Your double room has not dried. The paint must be inferior. I think it will never dry. And you have no view of the sea."

"That's bad," Mama said.

"Yes, very bad. But we have no other guests at the moment, so could you take two single rooms? At a discount?"

"No, we're used to sharing a room."

"Another little glass of sherry?"

"No, thank you. Absolutely not."

Le patron ran his hand over his head of stubby grey hair and sighed.

"So what do we do now?" Mama asked.

"We must think. Madame, one other possibility occurs to me, which is of course out of the question. I promised on the head of my dead wife never to rent out the house of the vanished Englishman."

"I understand," Mama said. "That is to say, almost. When did he vanish, this Englishman?"

"A year ago. But he sends the rent every month, quite correctly."

"And his address?"

"He never gives his address," *le patron* explained. "Perhaps he travels constantly. The stamps are from many countries."

"Irrational," said Mama appreciatively. "Is he old?"

"Not at all. Fifty or thereabouts."

"Lydia," Mama said, "I think we should go have a look at his house."

It was not far. The path ended in a white gate, beyond which was the Englishman's overgrown garden and, in its midst, a very small whitewashed cottage, covered with geraniums. Mama stopped abruptly and burst out, "The Secret Garden! Lydia, who wrote that?"

"Compton Burnett," said Lydia.

Everything in the garden was lush and verdant, especially the weeds. Rusty tin cans were strewn everywhere. The well was covered by a thicket of wild roses.

There was a look of dejection on Monsieur Bonel's heavy face. "The house is too small," he explained. "The water pipes don't always work. And you can't use the water from the well. Mesdames, I can only hope that the double room will dry as soon as possible."

"*Cher monsieur,*" Mama said, "I hope it never dries." She sat down on the edge of the well and looked him straight in the eye. "Monsieur, this is precisely what I'd been hoping for, although I didn't know it until now.

"But this area is not without its dangers for two single ladies."

Mama watched him, and waited.

Finally he said, rather curtly, "You shall have a protector, a small but unusually ill-tempered dog. I will borrow it from my neighbour Dubois. Its name is Mignon." He unlocked the door, gave her the key and added, "And now, Mesdames, I must make arrangements for your comfort."

Mama hung her hat on a nail beside the door.

Apart from a wide double bed, there wasn't much in the room – a table, a chair, a bureau. The walls were white and the floor was covered with red tiles. The Englishman had his hotplate in one corner, along with several wooden boxes labelled "Gordon's Gin" in which he kept his cooking utensils.

"We won't look in the bureau," Mama said. "We'll live out of our suitcases, we can be just as anonymous as he is! Now we're going to do everything very differently, that is to say …"

"Irrationally," Lydia finished the sentence.

"You don't like the idea?"

"Of course, Mama. That will be fine."

When they walked out into their garden the next morning, a little black-and-white dog rushed toward them barking like mad. He snapped at Mama's skirts, quivering with agitation.

"But he doesn't *like* me!" Mama squealed, and Lydia replied that maybe the dog had never seen women in anything but jeans or shorts, maybe skirts struck him as threatening.

"Good," said her mother. "I'll threaten him right back! And I will speak to *le patron* about this abhorrent little beast."

Monsieur Bonel had served breakfast for them in the special pergola reserved for the *pension's* double room. Red roses had been tucked into their napkins.

He hoped everything was satisfactory and that Mignon had behaved himself.

Mama didn't reply immediately, and when she finally spoke, to mention that her rose needed water, she sounded curt and not particularly pleasant.

"Everything is fine," said Lydia quickly. "And now we thought we'd go to the beach."

"Oh yes, the beach ...", *le patron* repeated and threw up his hands in a gesture of helplessness. The same old story that he knew so well – guests discovering that the beach was sealed off by the walls the luxury hotels had built to shield their guests. In the vicinity of Juan les Pins, there simply was no beach any longer.

Mother and daughter made the long walk down towards the sea and then continued along the walls. It began to grow very hot. Cars whizzed by and sometimes stopped at a gate or a driveway. At last they came to a narrow opening between the walls, a corridor that led down to the place where the working fishermen had their boats. Two rowing boats were tied to a little dock made of planks.

"Mama," Lydia said, "what would you say to a sight-seeing tour of Juan les Pins and Monaco?"

"Wait a bit," Mama said. "I've got an idea."

"Is it irrational?"

"You'll see. And stop being sarcastic."

That night, Mama woke her daughter and said, "There's a full moon. We're going to make an excursion out to sea. But before we leave, I want to ask you something. Have you ever been in a position where everyone worried about you?"

"No. Why would anyone worry about me?"

"Then I can assure you it's a very unpleasant feeling, like being rejected. Let me tell you the sort of thing I'd hear: 'We'll let her rest and take it easy.' In other words:

'So that we're left in peace and can do what we want!' Do you understand? They were so *worried* about me, oh my, yes ... ! Now don't say a word. What about that time you rowed out in the moonlight, secretly? Do you remember?"

"No, Mama."

"Oh yes, you do. You had a moonlight party at sea and later you said that I needed my rest and that was why I hadn't been asked along. Now let's go. I'll find that little path and we'll take a turn on the Mediterranean."

The rowing boats were still there.

"We'll take the little one," Mama said. They climbed into the boat. Lydia rowed for a while and let the offshore breeze drive them onward, further and further out. From here they could see the bright facades of the big hotels along the coast and, very faintly, could hear their music. The sea was black, and the moon made a sparkling path on the water. It was quite cold.

"Aren't you freezing?" Lydia asked.

"Of course I am. It's always cold at sea."

"We didn't know ..." Lydia began, but her mother interrupted. "You knew perfectly well. Yes, yes, you were showing respect, but in the wrong way. Do I have to get rebellious all over again at this age just because you were too obtuse to understand? Well, that's neither here nor there. You can row us back now."

Mignon met them at the gate, barking wildly. Mama leaned down and, with all her might, screamed at the dog, and it stopped barking. As far as Lydia knew, her mother had never before done anything so vulgar. But it was impossible to say if it was a scream of frustration or of triumph.

After that night, a peculiar, controlled animosity developed between the dog and Mama. Mignon no longer barked, he merely growled and bared his pointy little teeth. He never took his eyes off her. When she took a nap in the garden, Mignon slunk in under her chair and wouldn't let Lydia come near. Every time Mama woke up, they showed each other their teeth, she and the dog.

"Maybe it's good for him," she said. "Rather pleasant to hate someone now and then, don't you think?"

"Yes," said Lydia, "you may be right."

Eventually, of course, they did find a beach. It was very far away and was rocky and littered, but at least it was a beach. A big sign stated that the area was private, a future building site.

They went there every morning, spread out their beach towels across the rocks and watched boats with red sails pass by in the distance. Mama stuck her legs in the water and said, "There aren't any seashells here."

"No," Lydia said. "I've read that they're imported only for the season. They spread them on the beach for the hotel guests to find."

"Why don't you go swimming?" Mama said. "You came here to swim, didn't you?"

"I don't feel like it."

Near the shore, a little sailing boat floated lazily by, carrying a group of young people clearly having a good time.

"Swim out to them," Mama said. "Take some initiative!" And she waved at the jolly group with her toreador hat.

"Please, Mama, don't. Don't be so mischievous. In Barcelona ..."

"Yes, yes, yes, I know. Very strict and austere in Barcelona. But that was just one time!"

"So, then, what are you playing at now?" Lydia wondered.

Nothing further was said and the boat sailed on by.

Le patron served dinner in the pergola, always with fresh roses for the ladies. He liked to hover nearby, sometimes leaning against his huge white refrigerator, which had a place of honour beside the trellis. He stood and listened to their foreign language and rushed forward at the least sign that there was something they required, some glass or serving dish he could refill – or to enquire in a whisper about the quality of the sauce or the wine. For their sake, he had brought forward the traditional dinner hour in France by several hours. And he worried constantly that they couldn't afford to eat lunch. So now and then he appeared at their gate with a basket of some kind, covered with a white cloth, and told them it contained leftovers that would eventually be thrown out anyway. The basket was placed discreetly just inside the gate before he left.

One day after dinner, *le patron* took Lydia aside and asked her to step into the lobby – it was nothing important. He gave her a little box full of seashells and explained hurriedly that some tourists had left them at the *pension*. They had been in Greece. "But Mademoiselle, you understand, not all of them at once."

"Of course not," Lydia said. "Much better if she finds two or three at a time."

"And otherwise, all is well?"

"Thank you, *cher Monsieur*, all is well."

Lydia put the box in her bag. Later she removed a shell stamped with the words "Souvenir of Mykonos".

They continued going to the beach. By now they had been on the Riviera for ten days. Each day followed the same recurring pattern – squabbling with the dog, Monsieur Bonel's breakfast, the beach, a siesta in the Englishman's garden, dinner, and a long evening.

Then one morning came a telegram. *Le patron* had placed it beside Mama's coffee cup. She read it and said, "Terrible. They want me home."

"A death?" he whispered.

"Not at all. I've won a prize. I have to accept a prize."

"Money?" he asked hopefully.

"No," Lydia said. "Just an honour." And then she translated from the telegram. "For artistic achievement that has brought renown to our country in nations far beyond our borders."

"I won't go," Mama said. "But we must send a beautifully worded telegram."

Le patron drove them to Juan les Pins in his pickup truck and stopped at the telegraph office.

"Thank you, my friend," Mama said. "Don't wait for us. We'll make our own way home."

They went in and found the blank forms.

"Detained by ill health?" Lydia suggested.

"Absolutely not. You don't wire from the Riviera that you're sick. You do that from home."

"Are you sure? There's a short story by Somerset Maugham where someone gets sick and dies in a luxury hotel on Capri, and the coffin ..."

"Yes, yes, but that's fiction. Take a new form. First, thank you. Proud and happy and surprised and so forth. But what's my excuse? That someone else is more worthy of the prize?"

"No, that's impolite. And they might think it's just false modesty."

"And they'd be right," Mama said. "I can't think of anyone worthier than I. A long cruise?"

"No, no."

"But I can't just say that I want to be left in peace!" Mama cried. "It's too hot in here! I'm sick and tired of the whole business, and you're no help at all."

Just then a very elegant, grey-haired man came over to them and asked in Swedish if he could be of help in any way. "You're new here," he said, "and as it happens I live in this little community all year round. I know everything there is to know about Juan les Pins, and it would be a pleasure for me to offer some small tips to newcomers. My name is Anderson."

"How kind of you," Mama said. "Just give me a moment ... Lydia, write all that, you know, pretty stuff, and tell them I'm hoping for a good party when I come home. That's original."

"I'll write," said Lydia.

Mr Anderson escorted them to a bar, which, he told them, was the most fashionable one in town at the moment. Here – during the season, of course – one could see the most interesting people, both film stars and millionaires. Not to mention those who saved for years for a week on the Riviera. They could also be interesting – and touching. "Might I offer you a small sherry?"

"No," Lydia exclaimed. "Mama detests sherry!"

Mr Anderson gazed at her, astonished.

"Good, Lydia," Mama said. "You're making progress."

It was too hot, and her hat pressed on her temples. Mama listened distractedly to their host, who wanted to show them the casino in Monaco, it would give him great pleasure. She didn't feel well. Now and again people came by and said hello with cheerful nonchalance and then wandered on. A large woman in self-consciously slovenly clothes came up to them and said, "Hi, Toto darling, new protégées? Madame, such an original hat!"

"Thank you," said Mama, annoyed. "But it's too hot. It's impossible to breathe in here!"

"Darling," said the large woman, "what you need is a light, airy hat like a parasol. Pink would go beautifully with your white hair."

They went to an exclusive little boutique called Women's Dreams, where Mama bought a hat she didn't care for at all. It was so expensive that they had to promise to come back later with the rest of the money. Mr Anderson wanted to escort the ladies to their hotel, but Mama explained that they had decided to find some quiet place and write some postcards. They said *au revoir* and, when the coast was clear, Mama and Lydia took a taxi home.

After a while, Lydia said, "Mama, you're a snob."

"So are you, thank goodness, though you're still in the early stages. Absolutely unnecessary to let them know we're staying at a *pension*. I want to be anonymous, and keep people at a distance. Sometimes, I mean. And now don't say anything about the hat."

Monsieur Bonel met them.

"Madame," he said, sorrowfully, "you have purchased a hat. I hope you haven't encountered Mr Anderson. A new protector?"

"That dog is a nuisance," Mama said.

"It behaves that way because it finds you interesting," he said sullenly. "He is a very lonely dog."

The next morning, the beach was occupied by a lot of boys, swimming and diving for all they were worth. The fun they were having increased substantially when they caught sight of Mama's hat.

"Pay no attention to them," Lydia said. "We'll go down a little further."

"But they're laughing at me!" Mama cried. "They think the hat is ridiculous! Good. Excellent. It *is* ridiculous. Why didn't you stop me from buying it? But I never know with you." She walked on down the beach and sat down with her back to the water. After a while she said, "Why are you so quiet? Is there something wrong?"

"No."

"Aren't you having a good time? Is the money all gone?"

"No, no. But of course we can't stay forever."

"You mean because of your job?"

"Oh, Mama, please," Lydia said. "We don't fit in here."

Mama took off her hat. "I fit in wherever I happen to be."

"Don't take it off, you'll get sunburned. Anyway they've already seen it. It seems to me we've had our fun and it's time to go home."

"It seemed like a good idea," Mama said.

"I know. You're always having ideas, it's your little indulgence. How am I supposed to know when I'm supposed to help and when you want to be stopped?"

"And now we're fighting?!" Mama howled in dismay.

Several of the boys ran by, laughing, throwing little rocks in Lydia's direction. "Very pretty old girl!" they shouted.

"Let's go," Mama said.

Le patron met them at the *pension*. "The Englishman has telegraphed," he informed them brusquely. "He's coming back. I am in despair."

"When is he coming?"

"Today. At any moment. I am in despair."

"Yes, you said that. However, we are ready to depart in any case."

"Mama, don't say that!" Lydia cried. "We can stay as long as you like! If the double room has dried. Just tell me what you want to do!"

"You decide," Mama said. She really didn't feel at all well.

"A little welcome-home party for him?" Lydia suggested. "That would be just your style ... If I were you ..."

Mama interrupted her. "But you're not me, you're a completely different person. You've made it very clear that I decide too much. Very well. You decide."

Monsieur Bonel waited, stared out the window, shuffled aimlessly among his papers, and reflected with concern on how foreign languages can sound. You understand a little from tones of voice and silences, but nevertheless ... And he thought about these poor Scandinavians who lived where it was so cold and dark, which could explain a great deal ...

Suddenly Lydia stood up and said, "Monsieur Bonel. Would you be so kind as to call the airline and book two tickets? For tomorrow, if that's possible. We'll need to get our suitcases as quickly as possible, and the Dubois boys can take the dog home with them. Maybe they can help us move. And tonight we'll sleep in the double room, whether it's dry or not."

"Thank you, Mademoiselle. I will call at once."

"Wait a moment. I believe Madame spent too much time in the sun. Do you have a medical guide?"

"Only a brochure. For tourists."

Lydia read it and said, "Cold compresses. If it's sunburn, she should drink juice and salt water. By the way, we have an unpaid bill at Women's Dreams ... Mama, how are you feeling? I don't think it's anything serious."

"You never know. What was the name of that man who died on Capri? How did they get him home? Wasn't there anyone to worry about him?"

"Of course," Lydia said. "Now try to sleep for a while."

By evening, Mama felt fine and declared that she wanted to make a farewell visit to her garden. On their way there, they met the Dubois boys with Mignon. When the dog caught sight of Mama, he reared up on his hind legs with his nose in the air and howled.

Le patron explained. "He is not angry, he is grieving. He's going to miss you, Madame."

They sat down by the well and *le patron* opened his basket and served wine.

"Lydia," said Mama, "what about the hat?"

"It's been paid for."

"But where is it?"

"Dear Mama," Lydia said, "you'll never have to see it again."

"Madame," said Monsieur Bonel, "everything has been taken care of. Mademoiselle has thought of everything."

"Remarkable. Lydia, remember to look up the phrase 'changing of the guard' in our dictionary. It might interest *le patron*. But of course it's only a dictionary for tourists …"

The evening was cool and lovely. The garden looked more secret than usual.

"Mesdames," said *le patron*, "I have a message. The Englishman has wired again." He handed the telegram to Lydia and shrugged his shoulders. "You see. He's not coming after all. He's on his way to Egypt."

"Highly irrational," Mama remarked. "Too bad, actually. It would have amused me to meet him."

The next morning, Monsieur Bonel drove his friends to the airport in his pickup truck.

They returned to their own country just in time for the very beginning of spring. So they had spring twice over – if it's fair, that is, to count them both.

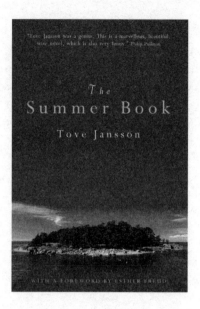

THE SUMMER BOOK

"*The Summer Book* is a marvellously uplifting read, full of gentle humour and wisdom." Justine Picardie, *Daily Telegraph*

An elderly artist and her six-year-old granddaughter while away a summer together on a tiny island in the Gulf of Finland. As the two learn to adjust to each other's fears, whims and yearnings, a fierce yet understated love emerges – one that encompasses not only the summer inhabitants but the very island itself. Written in a clear, unsentimental style, full of brusque humour, and wisdom, *The Summer Book* is a profoundly life-affirming story. Tove Jansson captured much of her own life and spirit in the book, which was her favourite of her adult novels. This edition has a foreword by Esther Freud.

"As smooth and odd and beautiful as sea-worn driftwood, as full of light and air as the Nordic summer. We are lucky to have these stories collected at last." Philip Pullman

A Winter Book

Tove Jansson

WITH A FOREWORD BY ALI SMITH

A WINTER BOOK

"As smooth and odd and beautiful as sea-worn driftwood, as full of light and air as the Nordic summer. We are lucky to have these stories collected at last." Philip Pullman

A *Winter Book* features thirteen stories from Tove Jansson's first book for adults, *Sculptor's Daughter* (1968), along with seven of her most cherished later stories (from 1971 to 1996). Drawn from youth and older age, this selection by Ali Smith provides a thrilling showcase of the great Finnish writer's prose, scattered with insights and home truths. It is introduced by Ali Smith, and there are afterwords by Philip Pullman, Esther Freud and Frank Cottrell-Boyce.

Tove Jansson | fair play

INTRODUCED BY ALI SMITH

FAIR PLAY

"So what can happen when Tove Jansson turns her
attention to her own favourite subjects, love and work?
Expect something philosophically calm – and discreetly
radical. At first sight it looks autobiographical. Like
everything Jansson wrote, it's much more than it seems ...
Fair Play is very fine art." From Ali Smith's introduction

What mattered most to Tove Jansson, she explained
in her eighties, was work and love, a sentiment she
echoes in this tender and original novel. *Fair Play*
portrays a love between two older women, a writer
and artist, as they work side by side in their Helsinki
studios, travel together and share summers on a
remote island. In the generosity and respect they show
each other and the many small shifts they make to
accommodate each other's creativity, we are shown a
relationship both heartening and truly progressive.

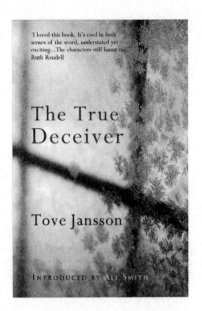

THE TRUE DECEIVER

"I loved this book. It's cool in both senses of
the word, understated yet exciting ... the
characters still haunt me." Ruth Rendell

In the deep winter snows of a Swedish hamlet, a strange
young woman fakes a break-in at the house of an
elderly artist in order to persuade her that she needs
companionship. But what does she hope to gain by
doing this? And who ultimately is deceiving whom? In this
portrayal of two women encircling each other with truth
and lies, nothing can be taken for granted. By the time the
snow thaws, both their lives will have changed irrevocably.

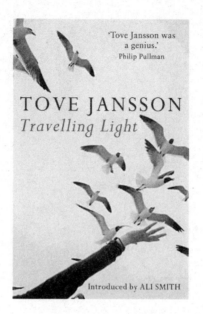

TOVE JANSSON
Travelling Light

Introduced by ALI SMITH

TRAVELLING LIGHT

"Jansson's prose is wondrous: it is clean,
deliberate; an aesthetic so certain of itself it's
breathtaking." Kirsty Gunn, *Daily Telegraph*

Travelling Light takes us into new Tove Jansson territory.
A professor arrives in a beautiful Spanish village only
to find that her host has left and she must cope with
fractious neighbours alone; a holiday on a Finnish
island is thrown into disarray by an oddly intrusive
child; an artist returns from abroad to discover that
her past has been eerily usurped. With the deceptively
light prose that is her hallmark, Tove Jansson reveals
to us the precariousness of a journey – the unease
we feel at being placed outside of our millieu, the
restlessness and shadows that intrude upon a summer.

TOVE JANSSON

ART
IN
NATURE

TRANSLATED BY
THOMAS TEAL

ART IN NATURE

An elderly caretaker at a large outdoor exhibition,
called 'Art in Nature', finds that a couple have lingered
on to bicker about the value of a picture; he has a
surprising suggestion that will resolve both their row
and his own ambivalence about the art market. A
draughtsman's obsession with drawing locomotives
provides a dark twist to a love story. A cartoonist takes
over the work of a colleague who has suffered a nervous
breakdown only to discover that his own sanity is in
danger. In these witty, sharp, often disquieting stories,
Tove Jansson reveals the faultlines in our relationship
with art, both as artists and as consumers. Obsession,
ambition and the discouragement of critics are all
brought into focus in these wise and cautionary tales.

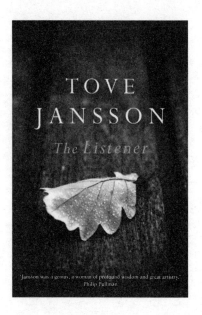

THE LISTENER

Aunt Gerda – the good listener – fears the encroaching
forgetfulness of old age. Her solution is to create an
artwork that will record and, inevitably, betray the secrets
long confided in her. So begins Jansson's short story debut,
a tour de force of scalpel-sharp narration that takes us
from a disquieting homage to the artist Edward Gorey, to
perfect evocations of childhood innocence and recklessness,
to a city ravaged by storms, or the slow halting thaw of
spring. These stories are gifts of originality and depth.